NO LONGER PR
SEATTLE PUBLI

"*Tongues of Flame* is well written an~~~ ~~~~~~~ ~~~~~~~d,
caring voice."   —*New York Times Book Review*

"Brown's words seem to come effortlessly, naturally off the
page."   —*Southern Living*

"Mary Ward Brown's stories are about old Southerners; not
really beached and not quite derelict, but with little room for
maneuver in the low water that remains after the tide has
mostly run out."   —*Los Angeles Times Book Review*

"Brown will be remembered for expanding the boundaries of
our knowledge about ourselves and how we write about
ourselves."   —Philip D. Beidler
The University of Alabama

"Mary Ward Brown extends the tradition of such powerful
20th-century writers as William Faulkner, Flannery
O'Connor, and Eudora Welty—writers who have demon-
strated and dramatized the tension between the inherited
social structure of the Deep South and its contemporary
disintegration."   —*Citation of the PEN American Center*

"With Mary Ward Brown's award-winning stories, Alabama
has at last built itself a house in Southern letters."
—*The Birmingham News*

Tongues of Flame

Tongues of Flame

MARY WARD BROWN

With an Introduction by
Jerry Elijah Brown

THE UNIVERSITY OF ALABAMA PRESS

Tuscaloosa

Copyright © 1986 Mary Ward Brown
Published in 1986 by E. P. Dutton/Seymour Lawrence
Introduction copyright © 1993 The University of Alabama Press
Tuscaloosa, Alabama 35487-0380
All rights reserved
Manufactured in the United States of America

2 4 6 8 9 7 5 3 1
02 04 06 08 09 07 05 03 01

Cover Design by Michele Myatt Quinn

Some of these stories originally appeared in these publications: "Good-bye,
Cliff" and "Tongues of Flame" in *Prairie Schooner* (Summer 1980 and Winter 1984); "The Amaryllis" in *McCall's* (July 1978); "Disturber of the Peace"
in *Grand Street* (Winter 1982); "Beyond New Forks" and "The Barbecue"
in *The Threepenny Review* (Spring 1982 and Spring 1983); "The Cure" in
Ascent (Vol. 8, no. 2, 1983); "New Dresses" in *Ploughshares* (Spring 1986);
and "Let Him Live" in *Shenandoah* (Summer 1986).

This is a work of fiction. Names of characters, places, and incidents are
either the product of the author's imagination or are used fictitiously, and any
resemblance to actual persons, living or dead, events, or locales is entirely
coincidental.
∞
The paper on which this book is printed meets the minimum requirements of
American National Standard for Information Science-Permanence of Paper
for Printed Library Materials, ANSI Z39.48-1984.

Library of Congress Cataloging-in-Publication Data

Brown, Mary Ward.
Tongues of flame / Mary Ward Brown ; with an introduction
by Jerry Elijah Brown.
p. cm.—(Deep South books)
ISBN 0-8173-0722-2 (pbk.: alk. paper)
1. Southern States—Social life and customs—Fiction. 2. Alabama—Social life
and customs—Fiction. I. Title. II. Series.

PS3552.R6944 T6 2001
813'.54—dc21   00-050778

For Kirtley Ward Brown

CONTENTS

INTRODUCTION
Jerry Elijah Brown

Mary Ward Brown's short stories provide their own introduction to the author's world, but for the reader wishing to test impressions a drive west of Montgomery on US Highway 80 toward Mississippi, preferably on an ordinary weekday morning, might also seem instructive. Signs of the Old South and this latest of New Souths loom up. To name a few: grim Selma, where racial progress seems reduced to endless bickering and historic old stores are abandoned, victims of recessions and suburban malls; exotic breeds of beef cattle grazing in lonely expanses of lush pastureland where cotton once grew; all-white, Christian academies and mostly black public schools. The pairings seem infinite, easy, and often grotesque.

If you've read Mary Ward Brown's fiction, however, you know these deceptively bold contrasts conceal layers of subtlety. In her stories, stereotypes, negative or positive, reveal their other sides, lighter or darker, and hasty, judgmental attitudes toward people and places do not last. Change and continuity, past and present, black race and white, massive abstractions and concrete particulars—all are reflected in a real, whole world, by characters from a complete social spectrum. Indeed, even if you are a Southerner or a student of Southern literature, you may conclude, as I and many others have, that this world cannot be fathomed by observers driving through it; in fact, the closest we are likely to come to understanding this particular part of America— and, by extension, our own lives in times of flux—is through the stories of Mary Ward Brown.

It would be hard to imagine a writer who knows this section of the South better. Mary Ward Brown lives about twenty miles from Selma, seven miles north of Highway 80, in the loosely defined community of Hamburg, in Perry County. In 1910, her parents, Thomas Ira and Mary Hubbard Fitts Ward, each with a son from a previous marriage, moved to the Black Belt from Chilton County, south of Birmingham, a region of small farms and peach orchards. Like enterprising immigrants in other parts of the country, they operated a store and lived upstairs. Their only daughter, Mary Thomas Ward (she is still called "Mary T." by her oldest friends) was born in 1917.

When she was about six, her father built an American Bungalow—style house about fifty steps from the store; he found the plans in a book and used heart pine grown on his own land and sawed at his mill. The house reveals much about the family's mindset. Although the Wards were successful merchants and farmers, they did not affect the airs of a fading aristocracy. No columned mansion, the white frame

Ward-Brown house has a New England look, with shingles across the second story and a porte cochere; a sleeping porch, added later, is the only distinctly Southern feature. The horizontal paneling inside has never been painted, and over the years the bare boards have mellowed to a warm brown. Though the rooms are small, light from the many windows gives the whole house a rich glow, setting off the antique furnishings, the hundreds of books and, in one upstairs room, the author's Macintosh word processor and laser printer. Aside from her early childhood and the seven years just after her marriage, the author has resided in this one house for more than six decades.

Her living still comes from the land, primarily the fifteen hundred acres she inherited of an estate that had grown to three thousand by the time her father died. Some of the fields she first saw white with cotton and black with people are now empty pastures, with wildflowers and shades of green that suggest impressionist paintings; ironically, these beautiful open spaces also signify a general decline in production and prosperity. Perry is one of the poorest counties in the state or nation. Of the 12,759 residents listed in the 1990 census, 8,192 are black, and more than half (4,628) are below the poverty level. Some form of public assistance goes to nearly one fourth of the households. Observations also reinforce this image of Perry County. Although vast tracts of land are available, skilled laborers are not, and jobs are scarce. The courthouse town of Marion, six miles north of the author's home, is crowded with cars on the day welfare checks arrive. Young people, black and white, who can make a better living elsewhere, do not stay in Perry County. And yet, however blighted the county may seem from these statistics and superficial observations, they do not tell the whole story.

Like most of the characters in her stories, Mary Ward

Brown started life in a stable world, and then saw it become a social, economic, and political roller coaster. She married Kirtley Brown (no relation to this writer) on her twenty-second birthday, one year after she had graduated from Judson College, a small Baptist women's college in Marion, and she left a place that seemed never to change. Brown, a Baylor graduate, directed public relations and student affairs for Alabama Polytechnic Institute, now Auburn University, located across the state near the Georgia line. Their son, Kirtley Ward Brown, was born in Auburn in 1942.

After her father's death, her husband decided they should move to Hamburg and farm the land themselves—though he knew nothing about agriculture—and she returned in 1946 to a culture soon to be shaken to its foundations. Cotton was giving way to cattle, and black people were moving off the land. Mary Ward Brown estimates that at one time about 250 black people lived in cabins scattered across her family's holdings. Now there are only cabin sites and no tenants.

During those first years the raising of grade Hereford beef cattle proved profitable, but then the market declined. The Browns had kept their land mortgage-free except for $10,000 on one small tract of land. They sold the herd, leased an easement for a natural gas pipeline, and paid off the mortgage, with $3,000 left over. (It is a point of pride to Mary Ward Brown that her parents' property has been clear of debt ever since.) Though beef cattle were no longer an option, the economy of the Black Belt took a surprising upturn. The soil that had grown cotton also suited soybeans, a crop lucrative enough to attract growers seeking land to rent. Suddenly, the Browns had a new breed of tenants, skillful farmers with their own massive equipment, who relieved the owners of the need to mortgage or to manage to the finest detail. Kirtley Brown, who on his own initiative had added a hundred acres to the estate, had returned to college administration as publications director at Marion Military Institute, but he contracted lung cancer and died in 1970. Though the rise in production costs and the drop in prices have made soybean raising less profitable, Mary Ward Brown still prefers to see rowcrops growing in the dark prairie soil that gives the section its name; unlike many other landowners, she has refused to surrender the land to pine trees. She continues to manage the farm and has herself added ten acres to the holdings.

Although the land is a central presence in her life, she has also always been fascinated with writing. As a child, she loved to "put things into sentences." At Judson, she studied journalism, which she respects because it taught her to be clear and concise. Although her carefully crafted stories are more than a news report from the New South, they do reflect a skilled writer who knows how to make every word count, who never digresses or drifts into obscurity, and who has great respect for a general public. If the stories transcend journalism, they are nevertheless not directed toward academic readers. She professes no interest in literary criticism; and, though she has lived all of her life near three colleges, she has never cultivated the society of literary scholars. Her primary interest is in writing and reading fiction, as anyone who visits her home will soon discover. Shelves of anthologies and copies of fiction-carrying periodicals—from *The Atlantic* to the *Threepenny Review*—point to a passion that the wider world began to discover after *Tongues of Flame* was published in 1986, when the author was in her seventieth year.

The book, which won the 1987 PEN/Ernest Hemingway Foundation Award for a best first work of fiction, reveals much about life in Perry County for a woman of Mary Ward Brown's station and generation but nothing about the author's efforts to learn her craft. She associates her itch to publish fiction with a sister-in-law, Margery Finn Brown, whose stories appeared in such popular periodicals as *Redbook* and *McCall's*. Margery passed along some how-to-write books, but it was not until Mary Ward Brown took a creative writing course at the University of Alabama in the 1950s (exact dates escape her) under John Craig Stewart that she discovered what she calls "theme," the backbone of a story that determines what can and cannot be included. Stewart's class met once a week, at night; she made sandwiches for an on-the-road supper, and her husband, weary from a day's work on the farm but doubtful of her driving skills, chauffeured, a round trip of 120 miles. She also took a creative writing course by correspondence from the University of North Carolina under poet Charles Edward Eaton. When she informed him that she wanted to write fiction, not analyze it, as a way of learning the short story form, he agreed, and he was the first to advise her to send her work to the literary quarterlies. Her first story was published in the *Kansas City Review* in 1955, but writing and her life as a mother soon came into conflict.

She recalls vividly a day when her son, then in junior high school, was shooting baskets outside with two friends and she was upstairs, absorbed in trying to write the ending to a story. "My conscience hurt me all the time," she said. "Kirtley had given up a good job to come out here on this 'dirt farm,' and I was shut up in a room trying to write fiction. I already had an agent, but there was my son, with his friends, and it was time to fix lunch. I thought I'd go crazy." She didn't. She made the lunch and stopped writing fiction for twenty-five years. Over that span, her son graduated from college and went to Vietnam (she wrote him every day), her husband died, and she managed the farm alone. After Kirtley Ward Brown finished law school, began his practice, and married, his mother took a job at Marion Military Institute, typing, cutting stencils, and tabulating test scores for the guidance counselor. Although she enjoyed working with students, she said she needed "a commitment of some kind." After she took a trip to Europe, she found it, a renewed interest in fiction writing that resulted in this collection.

Tongues of Flame was instantly popular. Though eight of the stories had been published earlier, the collection itself established Mary Ward Brown's identity. Readers across the country recognized not only a new Southern woman writer, but also one who had moved fiction into a world different from William Faulkner's or Flannery O'Connor's. Newspaper reviewers from Cleveland, to Kansas City, to Los Angeles formed a consensus, best expressed in the *New York Times Book Review:* "Though diverse in points of view and characters, each story deals in some way with a person who has been treading a path of inherited or habitual expectation and now, rounding a corner, discovers this is where the sidewalk ends. The character himself—or sometimes only the reader—is faced with the revelation that whatever is to happen now will have to be something new."

Not without honor in her own country, Mary Ward Brown found her work praised also by reviewers for newspapers in Atlanta, Montgomery, Birmingham, and even Greensboro, Alabama, a town eighteen miles west of Marion. The reviews generally were substantive and informed, not hollow patronizings. Putting Mary Ward Brown in the company of famous Southern writers but pointing out her distinctiveness, E. C. LeVert, reviewing for the *Birming-*

ham News (August 3, 1986), wrote that *Tongues of Flame* "serves notice of a quiet, craftsmanly attention to studied harmonies of scale, an art of understatement, enlivened by a sly sense of ornament." Critical acclaim resulted in a second printing of the collection, followed by a paperback edition, and within two years Mary Ward Brown faced the pain and pleasure of being a celebrity writer.

People Magazine came to Hamburg in 1988 and published a warm, insightful article about the book and the author's family life, complete with a page-wide close-up photograph of her in a straw hat, a smaller shot of her with her dog Boone, and a family portrait on the front porch, with Kirtley Ward, his wife Susannah, and their daughters Helen Ward and Mary Hays, then preschoolers. The author was awarded an honorary doctorate by Judson College and has been in demand at writers' conferences across the region. Though her obvious news value—the Deep South, farming, Episcopalian grandmother who struggles to pursue her craft and finally succeeds—and her graciousness with strangers continue to attract reporters, everyone who reads her fiction senses its essential toughness and realizes that it is guided by a powerful sensibility that moves through provincial matters to universal concerns.

That her fiction is more than quaint, local color—or veiled treatise—was recognized when one of these stories, "The Cure," was included for publication in *The Human Experience: Contemporary American and Soviet Fiction and Poetry.* The story is about an elderly black woman who refuses medical treatment from anyone but the retired, alcoholic white physician who has cared for her for years. A nonsentimental bond between the two results in a special communion, which the reader experiences without being led along by an intrusive omniscient narrator. The story is so free of political bias that an agent for the Soviet/American Joint Editorial Board of the Quaker US/USSR Committee, which edited the anthology, contacted Mary Ward Brown and asked if she were black or white. Understandably, a writer who winces at being called an artist but who wants to make "a piece of art you can live with, like a beautiful object" was pleased by the agent's question. She was especially delighted when, at a gathering of the contributors in Washington, fiction writer Anatoly Shavkuta said her story "is best, is best in book."

She has traveled to Russia, she has become adept at reading to audiences and being interviewed, and her work is now being published in new anthologies. Of more importance for those of us who've had our eyes opened by her stories, she continues to write. She rises at 6:00, writes till mid-morning, checks the mail, socializes with family and a wide circle of friends, manages her business, and is in bed by 9 p.m.

Reflecting on her life as a woman and as an artist, Mary Ward Brown says, in a characteristically flat tone of understatement, "I've had some of the best of both worlds—family and writing." Whatever hardships she might have endured in either world have made her neither blind nor bitter. Not one to ignore sorrow, she nevertheless has an eye for joy, whether it be in an old man's delight over a blossom or an old woman's pleasure over a vision of heaven. Disciplined, passionate, wise, acutely observant, and sympathetic to the broadest span of humanity, Mary Ward Brown is a writer whose stories belong in a library of classics. If you did not know that truth already, you shortly will.

Tongues
of
Flame

NEW DRESSES

Mrs. Lovelady, in a morning-fresh white uniform, helped Lisa's mother-in-law, Mrs. Worthy, into the car. Lisa could only stand by and watch. The bucket seat was too low and dangerously tilted for Mrs. Worthy as she was now, and Lisa wished she had listened to David, had come in his car instead of her own as he'd tried to tell her. Mrs. Lovelady kept smiling, for Mrs. Worthy's sake. Her eyes froze over when she looked at Lisa.

Mrs. Worthy had been a Laidlaw of Virginia, and before her illness she had looked it. Good clothes, her grandmother's jewelry, those quadruple-A shoes. Today she had on an old London Fog coat buttoned up to the chin. She was so thin it fell from her shoulders as from a hanger. On her head was a plain dark hat, to hide the loss of hair, Lisa supposed. She wore none of her rings. Only the yellow-gold wedding band she never took off.

Mrs. Lovelady handed in a cane with a wide silver band. "Got your medicine?" she asked.

Mrs. Worthy patted her purse and smiled. Her smile was too bright, like the wrong shade of lipstick.

Off at last, she didn't look back, though Mrs. Lovelady watched and waved from the walk. Behind Mrs. Lovelady was the portico of Mrs. Worthy's house, family home of her late husband. With its tall square columns and porches upstairs and down, the house stood as it had for over a century, through good times and bad, including wars that had cost the family a son in each generation. A driveway, where leaves and acorns crunched beneath the wheels of the car, made a deep half-circle in front.

It was the end of November, and trees on the grounds were all bare except evergreens. Several magnolias glistened in the sun. Their leaves, dull and suede-like underneath, shone as if waxed and polished on top. The sky was clear and blue, the air like a subtle stimulant. Nature seemed to favor this venture of Mrs. Worthy's, looked on by her son and her nurse as a whim of the sick, and foolish. But maybe it wouldn't kill her, David said.

They left the driveway for bare blacktop. A short stretch of woods, then a used-car lot followed by a veterinary clinic, and they were in the city limits of Wakefield.

"Why, there's Grandpa Robbins, out raking leaves," Mrs. Worthy said, with surprise. In front of a small neat house, an old man was at work in his yard. "I thought he must be dead and buried by now."

"Oh, no." Lisa laughed. "He was in the store just recently, buying something for another grandchild."

At mention of anyone's grandchild, Mrs. Worthy always fell silent.

For weeks Lisa had neglected, to the point of ignoring, her sick mother-in-law, but with an excuse that could pass for a reason. Lisa was the bookkeeper at Worthy's, the jewelry store Mrs. Worthy's son, David, had inherited from his father, to whom it had been left by *his* father, the first D. Worthy, Jeweler, of Wakefield. Lisa was born with a talent for figures, a gift as unmistakable as perfect pitch. In childhood she liked piggy banks, coins, and numbers, not dolls. Now, with the countdown to Christmas under way, she had a new computer at the store and could almost believe her own excuses.

Mrs. Lovelady had called last night during dinner. Mrs. Worthy had announced she was going shopping today, Mrs. Lovelady said. Alone, in a taxi. Mrs. Lovelady couldn't talk her out of it, so David would have to put his foot down, she said. To solve the problem and try to redeem herself, Lisa had offered to take her.

"Want to go by the mall?" she asked, near the intersection.

"Honey, no. Thank you." Mrs. Worthy was definite. "Just one stop for me. Miss Carrie is expecting me at Hagedorn's. She said she'd have some things picked out to show me."

"What did you have in mind?"

Mrs. Worthy seemed not to hear. She was trying to find the handle to the window.

"What are you shopping for, Mrs. Worthy?" Lisa asked again, in a moment.

"Oh, a dress." Mrs. Worthy looked off to the right. "Everything I own swallows me now."

In front of a red light, Lisa looked again at her mother-in-law. A year ago, she had seemed a different person. Off to work as a Pink Lady, gold earrings dangling from her pierced ears, she was talking, laughing, listening, busy in her church and the Charity League, running her own house. Now all that was over and Mrs. Lovelady was there, full-time. Behind them a bearded black man blew the horn of a Datsun. The light had turned green.

"Miss Carrie could have sent some things out," Lisa said, moving into the proper lane. "You could have tried them at home."

"But somebody would have to take them back, maybe try again. No, this will be easier. On everybody."

"Well, we have a beautiful day," Lisa said, with a smile.

It would be good to tell people, constantly asking, that she had seen Mrs. Worthy and had taken her shopping. "She's doing better, gaining a little weight," David had been saying lately, and she'd been repeating. Actually, Mrs. Worthy was no better at all and, if anything, worse.

Most of what David said Lisa didn't repeat. Health reports aside, it was the same in effect. His mother was a hero.

He had always praised her. "When we got home from school, she was there," he would say. Or, "Nobody could make hot rolls or mayonnaise like she could." Now his praise was on a different plane and Lisa heard it daily, her mother-in-law's courage, stoicism, self-sacrifice. After a day at the store, she heard it at night as she worked in the kitchen. Usually, she listened in silence.

"What do you mean, 'sacrifice'?" The words popped out one night, to her own surprise. "She has everything anybody could want."

His job was setting the table. Beside the sterling flatware he put down paper napkins. At first he said nothing, then his answer came like a blow in slow motion. "Not quite," he said, estranged already for several days to come. "She's sick, with nobody to look after her but a paid companion."

His mother came first with David, Lisa felt. She had thought so from the start, or almost the start. There had been a short happy time before she began to suspect that Mrs. Worthy sat on his right hand and she, Lisa, somewhere on the left. When she finally said so, in a burst of frustration, he was amazed.

"But she's alone now, and she's my mother!" he protested. "I love you both. Don't you know that?"

She didn't care about both. It was not to be shared. Something inside her was always watching for, ready to resist, any such notion on anyone's part.

David still referred to his mother's house as home, to their own home as "the house." "I'll run by home and see Mama, then meet you at the house," he began to say each afternoon as Mrs. Worthy grew worse. He also ran by on his way to work in the morning, and sometimes during lunch.

Mrs. Worthy was not to blame, Lisa knew. The bond had been forged too long ago and had nothing to do with her. Besides, Mrs. Worthy asked for nothing. On the contrary, she gave so much Lisa didn't like the obligations involved. Mrs. Worthy was a "giver," people said. Once the three of them had gone to church together, a weekly habit. At the family pew, Mrs. Worthy stood back for Lisa to enter first. When David in turn stood back for his mother, she motioned him ahead of her to sit by Lisa. Sunday after Sunday he sat between them, his eyes on the preacher with polite disinterest. Sunlight, coming through a stained-glass window, fell on him like a halo. His face between them, in that light, was fixed in Lisa's mind forever, she thought.

Hagedorn's, like Worthy's, had been family-owned for three generations. Lisa preferred Lowe's, which had a younger, newer clientele; but Mrs. Worthy did most of her shopping at Hagedorn's, and had for forty years. Lisa was relieved to find a parking place in front. When she came around to help Mrs. Worthy out, her mother-in-law was trying this time to find the handle to the door.

"I'm a real drag now, Lisa," she said.

Lisa wondered where she got the word, *drag*. Not from grandchildren that she wanted so much, and didn't have. Of the children she had brought into the world, only David was living. Her daughter had been killed in a teenage wreck, her other son in Vietnam. Now, since no one could take Lisa's place at the store, she and David were putting off children as long as possible, maybe altogether. They no longer even discussed it. Lisa had left the Catholic church and its birth-control laws. The Worthy family had been Baptist for generations, Southern Baptists, as unyielding on dogma as Catholics themselves. Lisa, a cradle Catholic, had felt she should join them.

"You'd give up your *soul* for him?" her father had asked, stunned, when she told him her decision. Later, in Wakefield, people would say, "She worships him." She should love her husband a reasonable amount, they seemed to think, and spread the rest around (family, friends, a good cause or hobby). When, in eight years, she had played no bridge, produced no child, joined no clique or club, they gave up on her. She was simply David Worthy's wife, "a girl from up north somewhere."

The windows of Hagedorn's were ready for Christmas, with formals and furs on one side, lingerie and robes on the other. While waiting for Mrs. Worthy to turn in her seat, to put one foot out and then the other, Lisa studied the display. Nice but dull, in her opinion. Nothing exciting in the least. The truth was, David carried out a similar policy at Worthy's. Lenox, Gorham, Waterford, diamonds in Tiffany settings. Lisa would like to add a little Steuben glass, a few pieces of costume jewelry by Dior or Chanel. Anything new and different, but no. "It wouldn't go over, love," he said. "This is Wakefield. And Worthy's."

Mrs. Worthy took a few steps, holding to Lisa's arm, and had to stop.

"Want to go back?" Lisa asked.

"No, give me a minute."

To avoid the looks of passersby, Lisa fixed her attention on the cane Mrs. Worthy leaned on. She had seen it before in Mrs. Worthy's back-hall closet, one of several left behind by members of the family. Someone's initials were engraved on the band, but all Lisa could make out was a central *W* through which other letters looped. When Mrs. Worthy first had to take over the big house and all the family relics, it was the last thing on earth she wanted to do, she once told Lisa. She had considered herself only an in-law at the time, she said. Now she took a deep breath and, still holding Lisa's arm, began to walk.

In the store everyone came up to greet her with hugs and handclasps. Everyone wanted to touch her, it seemed. On Lisa's arm, her hand began to tremble. "Thank you all, thank you." Her eyes filled with tears, but she rallied. "It's so good to see you! How *are* you?"

Lisa wouldn't have known the strain she was under, except for the telltale grip on her arm. She herself did not aspire to such grace. She was from Chicago, the daughter of an Irish contractor, successful, but self-made. When her mother died, he'd sent her to Catholic boarding schools and finally, against her wishes, to a sheltered college for women, near Wakefield. Sometimes at night, in the poster bed from David's old bedroom, the whole thing seemed more dream than reality—the Deep South like a foreign country, the Worthys with their contradictory piety and pride, the big house that was more than a house. Sometimes even David, behind the façade of manners and codes. Everything but the store where, surrounded by accounts and figures, she felt at home.

As a new wife she had wanted a new bed and had impulsively bought one, king-size, with her own money. David didn't say so, but she knew he wasn't thrilled. "We don't need all this room," he finally said. "Do we? I want you closer." She had put an ad in the paper and sold the bed, new bedclothes, all.

The elevator operator, a black woman, made Mrs.

Worthy laugh as they went up. "Pretty as ever," the black woman said. "Go buy you one them fur coats out the window!"

Miss Carrie, on the third floor, was a stout strawberry blonde, the color of her hair a little hectic today. In navy blue over a snug foundation, she was watching for her old customer when the elevator door opened. At first sight of Mrs. Worthy, the muscles of her face went slack, but she came forward smiling.

"Bless your sweet heart!" She took Mrs. Worthy's arm. "I'm so glad to see you. Let's go sit down."

Facing the elevator, near the center of the floor, a place was set aside for customers to wait, rest, and visit. Sofas and chairs were grouped around an Oriental rug. Tables held lamps and ashtrays, sometimes a potted plant or flowers from someone's garden. The spot, comfortable as the living room of a friend, was seldom without someone sitting there, purses and packages lying about.

Mrs. Worthy decided on a chair to sit in, and Miss Carrie turned to Lisa. "I'll take her now," she said, to Lisa's surprise.

"Yes, Lisa." Propped on her cane, Mrs. Worthy agreed. "Miss Carrie will help me. Thank you for getting me up here, my dear."

Lisa was dismissed. That she understood. Was she also being censured? Did everyone know she had not been attentive? Southerners were masters of indirection, she had found.

"When do you want me back?" she asked cautiously.

"Before long, I'm afraid." Mrs. Worthy swapped her cane for Miss Carrie's arm, and began the process of sitting down.

The black woman shook her head when the door was shut. "Lord, Lord," she said mournfully. "She going down fast now, and she so nice. I loves that lady."

Lisa knew what to say, but she stared at the floor and said nothing. No one could see her side at all, she thought, much less understand. So why care? In front of the store she checked her watch and, knowing she probably shouldn't, hurried down to Lowe's.

Lowe's too was ready for Christmas. Against a background of black and silver, like a starry night, one window featured evening gowns in shimmering holiday colors. Beaded, embroidered, winking with sequins. The spotlight, however, was on white, a crepe dress on a dais near the center of the window. Simple and Grecian, it was draped to one side and caught on the shoulder with a rhinestone clip, leaving the other shoulder deeply bare.

Ah! Lisa needed something new for the big Christmas dance. She had seen and liked the dress in a magazine, had even considered ordering it by phone. What a coincidence to find it at Lowe's! The only one, they said, but in her size and if she would wait, they'd get it from the window.

Lisa's regular salesgirl was off today. The one who brought the dress, whose name she didn't know, had large blue-green eyes, dramatically made up with lids like green satin. In a dressing room, she helped Lisa get the dress on, then stepped back to view it.

"You look like something for the top of the tree," she said.

Lisa studied her reflection in the mirror. The dressing-room lights put an overlay of gold on her medium-blond hair and skin. In white she did suggest, remotely, a certain concept of angel. But the dress was really Greek, its true association with broken columns and sculpture with blind, unfinished eyes.

"I want you to see that back, see the whole thing," the salesgirl said. With a motion like windshield wipers, her girdled hips led the way to a three-way mirror out on the floor.

In front of the mirrors a stylish older woman stood smoking, trying to make up her mind about a navy blue blazer she had on. She moved aside but not away and, with shaky fingers, raised the cigarette to her lips. While she exhaled, she looked at Lisa.

"That dress is out of this world on you," she said, coughing and choking. Ashes fell on her gray shoes like suede on suede.

David didn't always care for her clothes, Lisa knew, in spite of her efforts to please him. This time, for once, she was sure. He would love her in the white dress. She knew exactly how his eyes would look as he walked into the ballroom with her. The material, subtly draped, was as soft and light as air, the price more than she'd ever paid for a dress in her life.

"Think of it this way," the salesgirl said, as she helped take it off. "How can you afford *not* to get it?"

"I know." Lisa laughed. "I'd pay in regret, wouldn't I?"

She glanced at her watch, slipped on her skirt, and left the dressing room still buttoning her blouse.

The salesgirl was folding the dress for a large pink box with *Lowe's* in lipstick-red on the top. "Want this charged?" she asked.

"Yes, please, I'm Lisa Worthy. My husband . . ."

"Oh, I know. I know Mrs. Worthy, senior. How is she?"

"Not well at all." Lisa waited at the desk. "I'm on my way to pick her up now, and I'm late."

"Everybody in town is pulling for her," the salesgirl said, working faster. "She's such a doll, it's just not fair. Well. . . ." She handed the box to Lisa. "Thank you. Have a nice day."

Lisa hurried to the car and put the box out of sight in the trunk, so Mrs. Worthy wouldn't see it. Guilt, she supposed. Always guilt. Guilt on top of guilt. What she needed was to go to confession, and a wave of loss swept over her. She thought with longing of her rosary and missal and wondered where she had put them. She would hunt them up and use them. No one would know, and what if they did? At the thought, guilt gave way to resentment, toward what or whom she didn't even know.

In Hagedorn's she had to wait for the elevator, then got on alone. The operator, usually friendly and chatty, had nothing to say. Lisa hoped Miss Carrie, or somebody, had been looking after Mrs. Worthy. She would be worn out from waiting, but she'd be nice about it. They could go straight home and get it over.

When the door rattled open, she felt a deepening chill. Mrs. Worthy was asleep on a sofa, her chin on her chest, her hat askew. Beside her was a pearl-gray dress box.

Miss Carrie came forward with a swish of nylon-clad legs rubbing against one another. "She had to take a pain pill," Miss Carrie said, like an accusation. "It knocked her right out."

Lisa said nothing. Having hoped in vain for the best,

she was not prepared for this. Like a target moving toward the arrow, she approached her mother-in-law in silence. Every eye on the third floor was upon her, she knew.

"Mrs. Worthy?" she said softly, leaning down. Mrs. Worthy opened her eyes and held up her head. She looked from Lisa and Miss Carrie to racks of skirts and blouses, then walls lined with clothing beyond. "Oh, me, me, me," she said, pulling herself together. "Are we through?"

"Through, and had a nice little nap besides." Miss Carrie was breathing too fast. A pulse beat hard in the lap of her throat.

"I've come to take you home," Lisa said. "When you're ready."

Mrs. Worthy sighed. Her hands began to feel around for her purse.

"I have your things, ladylove." Miss Carrie held out the purse and cane. "I'll carry them down for you. Want a sip of coffee first? Would that taste good?"

Mrs. Worthy shook her head and Lisa wondered what to do about the hat, ludicrous at that angle. When she presumed to fix it, Mrs. Worthy paid no attention, like a child having its headgear adjusted.

"Ready?" Lisa picked up the dress box.

Mrs. Worthy had to be supported to the elevator, where the black woman averted her eyes and worked the controls in silence. Mrs. Worthy leaned on Miss Carrie, who kept one arm around her waist. Lisa stared blindly at advertisements taped to the wall, wondering what vanity or pride could prompt anyone so sick to subject herself, subject them all, to such an ordeal.

When the elevator stopped, Miss Carrie looked past Mrs. Worthy to Lisa. "I'll go on to the car with you," she said.

"Watch your step," the black woman cautioned.

Mrs. Worthy was plainly in no condition for farewells, and no one on the main floor approached her. The three women went slowly by a selection of nightgowns rising up as on kneeling ghosts above a long glass counter, their lace-trimmed hems arranged in swirls around them. They passed robes and caftans, slips and bras. Handbags lined a portion of the wall on their left, and a faint scent of leather hovered about. After costume jewelry and scarves, they finally reached the front. Someone was on hand to open the heavy double doors.

At the car Lisa and Miss Carrie lowered Mrs. Worthy backward into the seat. Lisa picked up her mother-in-law's legs, set them in place, and shut the car door. Outside the raised window, Miss Carrie tapped the glass and waved. Mrs. Worthy gave her a blank smile like a check she'd forgotten to sign, and sank back in the seat.

Lisa put down the windows and let in a rush of fresh air. Mrs. Worthy came to, to a degree.

"Those new pills are too strong," she said, frowning. "They put me to sleep sitting up."

Like the fullness of indigestion, Lisa's conscience rose up. She should take the blame and apologize, she knew; but she turned her head, let the wind blow her hair the other way, and said nothing.

"Did you find a dress you liked?" she asked, when the moment had passed.

Mrs. Worthy looked out the window. "I hope so," she said.

"It didn't have to be altered?"

"No, I decided not to bother."

Sick, sick, Lisa thought. Before, everything had to be right. For a quarter of an inch, a hem would be taken up or let down. Clothes had to fit but with ease; not too loose, but never tight.

The sun, straight overhead, fixed a blinding headlight on the windshield of each approaching car. Lisa lowered the visors on both sides, though Mrs. Worthy seemed not to mind the glare and stared ahead as if immune to it. Grandpa Robbins was no longer to be seen in the big yard he kept with such determination.

Beyond a wall of trees, mostly bare, the house finally came into view. Ready for the next hundred years, Lisa thought. For the rest of her life. She fixed her attention resolutely on the road. This time she drove on to the back, where the door would be closer, steps fewer, and came to a careful stop. Mrs. Worthy's Irish setter, Missy, was barking to announce them, so Mrs. Lovelady would be out to help any minute.

"Home again," Lisa said, with relief. Mrs. Worthy smiled and said nothing. All morning Lisa had wondered at her patience, like that of the poor, who could sit and wait for hours. An effect of the pills, she supposed. She turned to the box on the backseat.

"Mind if I look?"

For a split second, Mrs. Worthy didn't answer. It was as if a burst of glare to which she was not immune had suddenly struck her in the face. "Of course not," she said, when it passed.

Lisa held the box between them and lifted the top, then the crisp tissue paper. To her surprise she saw crepe de chine with tucks and lace, in a dusky shade of rose. She'd been expecting something else, an ordinary dress for trips to the doctor.

"Beautiful," she said, impressed but puzzled.

"We used to call that color 'ashes of roses.' " Mrs. Worthy gave a quick, light laugh. Humor flared up in her eyes like small flames.

A vision of absolute stillness flashed before Lisa, the rose dress on a background of tufted white satin. Staring at Mrs. Worthy, she felt the blood drain from her face while her heart seemed to rise up and flop over like a large fish. In the open box, tissue paper waved and shook from the trembling of her hands.

She knew that Mrs. Lovelady had appeared off to one side, that Mrs. Lovelady was speaking, perhaps to her. Unable to respond, as in a nightmare, she went on staring at her mother-in-law as if she'd never seen her before, as if what she saw was not a face but a revelation, not to be taken in all at once, in the blinking of an eye.

T H E   C U R E

When Ella Hogue continued to grow worse, her daughters all came home. Bee came first from nearby Vilula, then Andretta from Fort Wayne, and Lucindy from Miami. For two days and two nights they took turns sitting by the bed, waiting for the end. On the third day Ella began to improve. Consciousness came back first, then gradual alertness. Unbelieving, her daughters gathered around her.

Ella looked at them and sighed. "I ain't dead yet?" she said.

"Course you ain't dead!" Lucindy scolded. "You 'live as anybody. You done got better."

"I don't want to be no better," Ella said, "if I can't get up and do, like everybody else."

She lay beneath a quilt she had pieced and quilted years ago, in a bed given to her by Doll's grandmother. The bed was of solid dark wood, with a high carved headboard and cracked foot. White women hunting for antiques had wanted to buy it, or swap her something for it, for years. When her daughters arrived, the bedclothes had been dingy, and stale as the inside of the trunk where she kept them. Now the sheets on her bed were aggressively clean. The quilt had been aired in the sun. Ella's old head, tied up in a snowy rag, made the only dent in her pillow.

"You soon *be* up, Mama," Lucindy said positively. "You coming back thisaway!"

"How long you been here, Cindy?" she asked. She was too weak to move.

"I come Tuesday," Lucindy said. "Soon as Bee called up, I told my boss-lady, 'My mama sick in Alabama and I got to *go*.' Then I got on that bus!"

Lucindy was Ella's oldest, born the first year after puberty when Ella was barely fourteen. Her large frame, heavily fleshed through the hips and bust, was bony elsewhere. Zipped and buttoned into a red polyester pantsuit, she was like a Christmas stocking half filled with fruit. Her hair was a vigorous iron-gray, and her aging face was pleasant.

"I'm here too, Mama," said Andretta, who had been in Fort Wayne so long she talked like a Yankee. A copper-colored replica of Ella at the same age, Andretta leaned down to touch her mother's still, unresponsive hand.

"I see you, Retta," she said, and smiled.

Bee's presence was taken for granted. She was a mixture of her two half sisters, smaller and lighter in color than Lucindy, larger and darker than Andretta. Lucindy and Andretta were both "outside" children, but Bee had been born and raised in wedlock. After Bee there were no more, girls or boys, because Ella's husband had had mumps that went down on him.

"What got the matter with me?" she wanted to know.

"You had a little sinking spell, is all," Andretta said. "You over it now."

"I don't know nothing about it."

She turned her face toward the open door. She did not even know what month it was. Clusters of yellow berries were on the chinaberry tree, so it had to be fall. Across the road, mock oranges were green and a few lay on the ground.

A small fire burned in the fireplace. Bee began rattling lids on the stove in the kitchen and soon there were smells of cooking and smoke, but Ella felt no hunger. She felt nothing at all, except the faint presence of life itself.

"Has Doll been here?" she asked.

"Every day," Lucindy said proudly. "She be back after while. She don't know you done come to."

Bee pulled up a chair and sat down by the bed with a cup of hot soup.

"Take a sip of this, Mama," she said, holding out a spoon half full.

Ella waited, then took a small taste. The soup was chicken with soft rice. When Bee held out the spoon again, she let herself be fed and kept on sipping until the spoon scraped bottom.

Afterward she closed her eyes and rested, listening to the girls tiptoeing around, whispering so as not to disturb her. She felt like dozing off, but first she had to attend to something.

"What time she coming?" she asked.

"Who, Doll?" Bee said. They had sat down around the fire to eat. "Why? You want her?"

"I wants her to get Dr. Dobbs to come work on me," she said, "and get me up from here."

All three women turned to look at her. Bee swallowed the food in her mouth, field peas, sprinkled with hot-pepper sauce, and corn bread.

"Dr. Dobbs *been* retired, Mama," she said carefully. "He ain't doctored on nobody in three-four years. I think he even kinsa mindless now."

"Thas all right," Ella said. "I ruther have him mindless than them others. Dr. Dobbs know how to move my bowels and flush out my kidneys, and get me back on my feets."

"He could years ago, Mama, but he can't do nothing now. Your bowels can't move, noway, until you eat—and you ain't et until just now."

"Who made that soup?" she asked.

"I did, Mama," said Andretta. "Was it good?"

"It needed mo' salt," she said.

They looked at each other and smiled.

"One of y'all go tell Doll I wants to see her," she said in a clear, strong voice, and all smiles vanished.

Each time someone knocked on the door, Sally Webb thought it was bad news about Netta (her childhood

name for Aunt Ella), who had lived on the farm and
worked for Sally's family most of her life. Though she
dreaded Ella's passing with all her conscious mind, Sally
was dimly aware of a subterranean impatience to get it
over and behind her, for things to get back to normal,
whatever the cost.

Both Sally's parents and all the other old people,
black and white, who had lived on the place were now
dead and gone. Ella had hung on, puttering around her
house and yard, last not only of her generation but of a
whole era.

She never asked for anything. On the contrary, she
was always coming up with a jar of jelly, a bunch of
greens, or a sack of something. Still, Sally felt responsi-
ble for her, down there alone. When she hadn't seen her
out for several days last week, she had stopped to find
her in bed, slightly disoriented. She had called Bee, who
came in a dented old car and took Ella to the doctor. Dr.
Cox reserved a bed in the hospital, but once out of his
office Ella refused to go. Bee brought her home and came
to get Sally.

Ella lay on top of the covers in her old-fashioned
Sunday clothes and lace-up, size-five shoes.

"Dr. Cox wants you in the hospital, Netta," Sally
explained, "where they can get you well. Bee and I don't
know what to do for you, like they do."

"Yes'm." She looked off to one side. "I be all right
here."

"But Bee needs to get back to work," Sally insisted.
"There's nobody to look after you here."

"I don't need nobody," she said. "The Lord be with
me."

Sally looked at Bee, who looked helplessly back.

"Well, you have to go, Netta," Sally said firmly. "You need medical attention. Now, I'm going back to call the hospital while Bee packs your things. Bee and I will go with you, and stay as long as you need us."

Ella's face was a mask, stoical and lonely. When tears suddenly stood in her eyes, it was as though a wood carving started to weep. She turned her head and a tear fell off on the pillow.

"I wants to die at home, Doll," she said.

So Sally called the cafeteria where Bee worked and told them Bee would have to be out for a while. She talked to Dr. Cox on the phone and went to town for medicine. When Ella continued to grow weaker, Bee came up and called the others. Ella would not know now whether they took her to a hospital or not, but no one suggested it. Sally reported to Dr. Cox each day. Ella's daughters turned her frequently from one side to the other as he'd instructed, and kept her clean. It seemed a matter of time to the end.

Now it was Lucindy who knocked on the door, but Lucindy was smiling.

"Mama done woke up and et," she said. On the underside of the announcement, like an insect behind a sheer curtain, was a hint of disappointment.

"Well, thank the Lord," Sally said.

"Yes'm, but . . ." Lucindy would not come in the door Sally held open. "Now she want you. She want you to get Dr. Dobbs to come see her."

"Dr. Dobbs! Why, he's senile and alcoholic too, they say."

"That's who she want, though."

"Wait a second." Sally went back for her keys and a sweater.

The moment she saw Ella alive and conscious after days beyond reach, her heart seemed to crowd the walls of her chest. Standing by the bed, she looked down at the slight figure beneath a quilt in which were sewn scraps from her own school dresses.

"You go'n get Dr. Dobbs fuh me?" Ella asked.

"I'll do my best, Netta," she said.

Dr. Dobbs sat bolt upright in the front seat of the car, beside his black driver, Elmo. A beard of fat hung down around his face, which was mapped with forking red and purple veins. Pale blue eyes stared out as from the raw white of an egg, in a look of fixed displeasure. He wore a dark suit of lightweight wool, a white shirt, and a striped silk tie. A large stomach pushed out against the buttons of his coat.

Sally was waiting on the porch when they drove up, and she hurried out to the long, black sedan.

"I'm Sally Webb, Dr. Dobbs," she said, when Elmo let down the window. "William and Mary Ann Webb's daughter. I'll ride down to Aunt Ella's with you."

"Get in, young lady," he said. "I wish I could assist you."

"Aunt Ella must be nearly ninety now," Sally said, speaking up from the backseat. "But she thinks you can help her."

He seemed not to hear. Instead he turned his head from one side to the other, looking at a dilapidated cotton gin on the left and leaning seed house on the right.

"This place looks run down," he said. Each time he spoke an essence of alcohol filled the car as though sprayed from a bottle.

"Well, things have changed since my father's time, Dr. Dobbs," Sally said. "The cattle business is off, and there's nobody to clean up and patch up the way there used to be."

"Where's all the niggers?" he asked.

"Everything is done with machinery now," she said quickly. "Most of the black people have gone."

"Good riddance," he said. "I wish they'd all leave—go back to Africa. Except Bojangles, here. Wadn't for him, I'd be up the creek without a paddle."

Sally said nothing.

"What's the name of the old nigger woman?"

"It's Ella Hogue, Dr. Dobbs. Aunt Ella. She cooked for us and was your patient for years. You used to like her pecan pies."

"I don't recall," he said.

At Ella's house, a two-room cabin by the side of the road, Elmo helped the doctor from the car as though midwifing a birth. Once on his feet the old man was handed a cane, but his balance was yet to come, by degrees. Glaring about him, he waited.

"Somebody get my bag," he said at last, then fixed his attention on walking.

At the porch steps he turned himself over to Elmo again, and a new struggle began.

Lucindy, Andretta, and Bee, freshly washed and dressed, stood in the open doorway. For the trip home,

Lucindy and Andretta had each brought black outfits for a funeral, and not much else. Now they wore the same clothes, rinsed out and dried overnight, in which they had arrived.

"Good morning," the old man said formally. "I'm Dr. Dobbs, and this is my companion, Elmo Green." There was a ripple of greetings, all ending in "Doctor."

"Where have you got the patient?" he asked.

"Right here, Doctor."

The women backed into the room that had been thoroughly straightened, dusted, and swept. An empty cane-bottomed chair had been placed by the bed. In the middle of the room a hanging light bulb was turned on, and a kerosene lamp on the dresser had been lit. Clean, starched cloths, made of bleached feed sacks edged in coarse lace, covered the tops of the dresser, trunk, and one small table. A low fire burned in the fireplace, the hearth freshly brushed with Ella's sedge broom.

Dr. Dobbs made his way to the bed and propped his cane against the wall.

"Well, my old friend." Holding on to the head of the bed, he leaned down and shook Ella's hand. "How are you?"

"Pretty low, Doctor," Ella said. "Pretty low."

He turned to the onlookers. "If you will all step outside now," he said, "I'll examine the patient."

First he moved the chair closer to the bed, so close it touched the mattress sideways, and sat down carefully. Then he picked up Ella's wrist, found her pulse, and took out a heavy gold watch on a chain. Counting with his lips, he watched the second hand jerk around its tiny course.

Light played along the watch chain as his stomach rose and fell.

Ella's eyes followed with profound interest as he opened the bag on the floor, took out a stethoscope, and adjusted it in his ears.

"Open your gown, please," he said.

Ella did not recognize the gown they had on her. She could not find the opening.

"Pull it up from the bottom," he said. "You still remember how to do that, don't you, Auntie?"

"Doctor!" she said, and laughed in spite of everything.

He placed the metal disc on the left side of her chest and looked away while he listened. He moved the disc several times. He had Ella turn on her side and listened from the back.

He took her blood pressure, squeezing the bulb and waiting, squeezing and waiting. With a light, he looked into her eyes, ears, and nose. He felt the glands in her neck.

Finally he leaned back in the chair and called out, "Elmo!"

Elmo appeared in the doorway. "Sir?"

"I need to stand up," the doctor said.

Elmo came forward to pull him up by the arms like a monstrous baby.

"Now stay there and help me," he said.

Elmo stood behind the doctor, reached beneath his coat, and gripped his belt firmly. As though holding a large fish on a line, he looked the other way while the doctor palpated Ella's stomach and pushed back the covers to press her ankles for swelling. He examined her

feet, one at a time, flexing them up and down and from
side to side.

"Do your corns bother you much?" he asked.

"No sir. Not much," she said. "Just when it rains."

Ella helped him pull the covers up. Elmo lowered
him back into the chair and went out, closing the door
behind him.

The doctor rested for a moment.

"What you've got, Auntie," he said, "is the same thing
I've got—old age. There ain't but one cure for it."

"Sir?"

He spoke a little louder. "I said I can't cure you—but
I can get you back up for a while."

"I knowed you could, Doctor. That's why I sont for
you. I don't want to be a burden on nobody."

"That's what we all say." He began putting instru-
ments back in the bag. Leaning over squeezed off his
breath and he said no more, though Ella listened and
waited. When he took out a prescription pad and began
to write, she raised her head from the pillow.

"Doctor, I hope you put down that tonic used to hep
me so much," she said.

"Tonic?" He stopped to think. "That was Vinatone,
probably. In a sherry base." Suddenly he looked at her
with new interest. "Hold on. Wait a minute. Now I recall!
Ain't you the one used to make that good muscadine
wine?"

Ella's eyes gleamed in the lamplight. "Scuppernong
too," she said.

"Well, bless my time! It was the best in the country."
His eyes opened wider. "Have you got any left?"

"Just call one of my girls, Doctor," she said.

"Hey, girl!" he called out, making his stomach heave. "One of you . . . ladies!"

Bee hurried in, plump and womanly. Her face was serious.

"Bring one of them jugs out the kitchen, Beatrice," Ella said. "And a clean glass."

"Bring two glasses, if you don't mind, Beatrice," the doctor said.

They stood in the yard and waited, until Sally began to feel awkward.

"I'll go on home, Elmo," she said. "Stop and blow at the house when you start back. I'll come talk to Dr. Dobbs and get the prescriptions."

When she had gone, the others sat down on the edge of the porch, two on each side of the steps, their feet on the ground. Elmo sat beside Andretta.

"Doll sho favors her mother, don't she?" Lucindy said.

"But she got ways more like her daddy." Andretta's speech had lapsed. It was now almost as southern as the rest.

Bee yawned. A sleepy midday pall had settled over them like a spell in a fairy tale. The air was pure and still. Even the birds were quiet. There was no sound except insects saying their mantras, out of sight in the trees and grass.

"He takes his time, don't he?" Lucindy said, at last.

Andretta looked at her wristwatch. "He been in there thirty minutes now," she said.

Bee got up, eased to the door, and peeped through

the crack. When she turned away, she was grinning. "They in there sleep, both of 'em," she said, and sat back down. "He bout to fall out the chair."

"Lawd . . ." said Lucindy.

"Jesus!" said Andretta.

Lucindy turned to Elmo. "What us go'n do, just wait till he wake up?"

"It won't be long," Elmo said. "He soon have to make water, drinking all that wine."

Bee and Andretta chuckled. Smiles lingered on their faces, but Lucindy was frowning. "Reckon will he do her any good, though?" she asked.

"If anybody kin, he will," Elmo said. "He a good doctor, and he ain't forgot his learning. He still reads all them books and papers we gets in the mail."

"How long you been with him, Mr. Green?" Andretta asked.

"Three years, last month. I started off just driving him. Then his wife died and my wife left me, so now I stays with him twenty-four hours a day."

"Is that right?" said Bee, from the other side of the porch.

"He old and fractious," he said, "but he don't mean nothing by it. He ain't even woke, 'cept in the morningtime. And we got a cook to wait on us, and all. He got plenty money."

"Not changing the subject," Lucindy said, "but what us go'n do now, y'all? She can't stay by herself no longer."

"One of us just have to stay with her," Andretta said. "Or take her home with us."

"And that would kill her in a hurry," Bee said. "She

done already cried and told Doll she want to die at home."

"Y'all could hire somebody to stay with her, like me," Elmo teased.

"Chile, we ain't no rich doctors," Lucindy said, and they laughed as though harmonizing, their voices weaving in and out of one another before fading into silence.

Andretta sighed. "I'd never find a job down here good as the one I got up there," she said.

"Old as I is, I couldn't find no other job a'tall," Lucindy said. "But if anybody stay, it ought to be me. I'm the oldest. I'm old enough to be y'all's mama myself."

"I'm the closest, though," said Bee.

Elmo turned to Andretta. "Maybe you ought to relocate yourself, Miss Andretta, and come on back home."

She gave him a sidelong smile. "Why? You go'n still be round?"

"One thing we *ain't* go'n do," Bee said, "is put her in no nursing home."

There was instant agreement. "Naw!"

"I tell y'all something. . . ." Lucindy looked off through bare trees to the wide, impersonal sky. "Old age is *bad*."

"You ain't wrong," Andretta said slowly.

They sat in silence until Lucindy's stomach began to growl, so loud that everyone smiled. "You hush!" she said, and hit it lightly with her hand.

The sun had reached high noon, and though the porch shaded their bodies, it shone hot on their feet and legs. A housefly buzzed around first one and then the other, to be brushed absently aside. Now and then a leaf wandered down. Faced with changes as yet undefined, the women examined their thoughts without speaking. All three were grateful their mother had not died, but her living would be costly from now on. If one stayed, the other two would have to pay for it.

Elmo kept politely quiet, his eyes fixed on the road. Like actors on a stage, they waited for the old man to call out and let the ending begin.

THE BARBECUE

When Tom Moore saw Jeff Arrington come into his store and start back to the fireplace where he was, he braced himself. What does he want now? he wondered.

It was midmorning and Tom was sitting with a representative of the Power Company, there to negotiate a right-of-way across Tom's land. They were drinking Coca-Colas from sweating green bottles.

Since it was May there was no fire in the fireplace, but people sat around it all year. Smokers used it for an ashtray and chewers spat in it. Everyone used it as a wastepaper basket. Tom's black clerk, Willie, cleaned it out the first thing each morning when he swept the store. Over the mantel hung a wall clock in an oak case, its pendulum swinging back and forth hypnotically. The tick seemed to make babies stop crying and old people doze.

Jeff nodded to Tom's wife, Martha, busy behind the counter. The store was longer than wide, with groceries on one side and dry goods on the other. Martha was the main clerk and Willie her assistant. Tom helped out on Saturdays, and whenever he was free. He also had the farm to look after—plus business, as now.

At fifty-five Jeff still looked young. His hair was cut by a stylist, not a barber, and one side fell over his forehead in a boyish bang. He was over six feet tall and, except for a low stomach that pushed his belt down to hip level, had kept the rangy thinness of his youth. As usual, there was a half-smile on his face. At the fireplace, the smile expanded.

"How y'all today?" He held out his hand to the Power Company man, a stranger. "Jefferson Arrington," he said, and took a chair across from Tom's.

The chair was of unfinished wood with a cane bottom, like others for sale in the store, along with work clothes, patent medicine, nails, rattraps, and whatever else might save people in the surrounding area a ten-mile trip to town while making a profit for Tom.

"Nice weather," Jeff went on. "I hope it lasts through the weekend."

The Power Company man laughed. "You must not farm, then. The farmers need rain."

"No, I'm a lawyer. I've got a camp house down the road, but I live in town."

"Any kin to Dave Arrington, used to be in the legislature?"

"He was my father," Dave said proudly. "I'm named for him. You knew him?"

"Just knew of him."

"Yes—he was the second, I'm the third, and my son Dave is the fourth."

"What can I do for you, Jeff?" Tom asked, to get it over.

"I'd like to use your phone, Tom, if you don't mind." Jeff lit a cigarette and threw the match in the fireplace. "I've got a pig and a lamb to barbecue Sunday night, and I need to call a few people."

Behind Tom's glasses one eye, of a somber blue, seemed locked in a different direction from that of the other eye, as if trying to see the bridge of his own nose. His good eye looked coldly at Jeff.

"Help yourself," he said.

Jeff had inherited money, securities, the antebellum house he lived in, and rental property all over town; but his renters told of falling plaster, leaking roofs, and dangerous gas heaters. Everything he owned was now mortgaged, sometimes more than once, according to people in the courthouse. He walked off to the office as if walking were a form of recreation.

Tom turned back to the Power Company man. This man had no authority. All he could do was repeat an offer already rejected. Time was money, Tom had learned long ago, and not to be wasted. From his pocket he took an inexpensive watch like the ones he kept in stock, looked at the time, then glanced up at the clock.

"You'll have to excuse me today, sir," he said. "That clock is slow, and I've got to get something in the mail."

The store had been built in 1890, the heart of a small community little changed except for paved roads, electricity, indoor plumbing, and new generations of the same families. The office, on the other side of the fireplace wall, was used for paying the help, bookkeeping, and business too complex to be transacted at the fireplace. On one side of the room was a stand-up desk with a square homemade stool that had come with the building when Tom bought it, thirty years ago. Jeff sat on the stool smiling into the telephone, inviting someone to his barbecue.

"Come early," he was saying, "in time for a drink."

At another, newer desk across the room, Tom uncovered an electric typewriter and inserted a sheet of stationery with the letterhead *Moore's Farm & General Store.* Using two fingers, he rapidly typed in the date.

Jeff turned with his hand over the mouthpiece. "Does this bother you?" he asked—a formality, Tom knew.

He shook his head as expected.

To his daughter, Laura, at Vanderbilt, he wrote, "My dear girl:—Kathy's Daddy using phone so I'll cut this short. Mother and I alright. No rain in three weeks. Nothing in the way of news. Call us Collect when you have time, and don't forget your old Dad. Allowence enclosed."

From the pocket of his shirt, he unclipped a pen and signed his name, Thomas J. Moore, as to anyone else.

Jeff was named for the southern hero Jefferson Davis. The first time someone told Tom his weekend neighbor was a collateral descendant of the president of the Confederacy, of the same blood and could trace it, Tom had laughed. "You mean they got the papers on him, like a bull?" Laura said there was an original portrait of President Davis's mother in one of the Arrington parlors. They prized it above everything else in the house, she said.

The *J* in Tom's name stood for Jefferson too. He was named for a hero even greater, the architect of American democracy, but he was no kin whatsoever. It was just a name his father had picked out, hoping it would help him amount to something, his mother said. His father had been a two-mule farmer in the poorest county of the state.

He wrote Laura's check and addressed an envelope.

"Better get that on in the box," Martha said, when he came out of the office. "It's time."

She was selling Minit-Rub to an old man in a felt hat, shapeless and faded from wear in all seasons. Willie was weighing bananas for a black woman with a baby. Outside a car, then a truck, pulled up for gas. While Tom filled the tanks, both drivers got out and went inside. The truck driver was eating sardines, hoop cheese, and crackers off the counter when Tom went back in. It was an ordinary busy morning.

Before the noon rush, Willie went next door to Tom's house, where the cook's job was to have a hot meal waiting. Tom and Martha would take turns going later.

No one was left in the store except Tom, Martha, and Jeff—still on the phone in the office. For the first time all day Martha sat down, on a stool behind the cash register. Tom walked up to stand in front of her while looking over the front page of the newspaper.

Jeff came out in an obvious hurry. When he glanced at the clock, he began to walk faster.

" 'Preciate it, Tom, Mrs. Moore." He lifted one hand in a gesture of farewell. "I've got to run now, but thank you!"

Martha smiled politely. Tom looked up from the paper with no change of expression. He watched Jeff hurry out the front double doors. A white Mercedes started up outside.

"How much does he owe?" Tom asked.

"Too much." Martha picked up a Popsicle wrapper and dropped it in a wire basket behind the counter. "I just looked it up."

"When you send his bill next month, I'll dun him."

She said nothing for a moment, then asked offhand-edly, "He didn't invite us?"

"To his barbecue?" Tom looked at her in surprise. "Did you think he would?"

She made no reply.

"He didn't think of it, I guess," he said. "We don't belong with that crowd."

"But he used our phone to invite them."

After thirty-five years, he still didn't understand her. It had never entered his mind that Jeff would invite them. They wouldn't go if he did. They never went any-where at night, except to bed. They had to get up and work the next day. What did she want—a chance to say no?

"You're just sensitive," he said. "He didn't mean to slight us. He just never thought of it, that's all."

"That's even worse," she said. "If he didn't think of it, we don't count at all to him. We're just nobody."

Like him, she had had few advantages growing up, but she was a remarkable woman. Everyone liked her, praised her. He could never have accumulated three thousand acres of prime Black Belt land without her. What did she care about a barbecue?

She did though. It was in her eyes.

He walked to the front door, looked out, and came back.

"I'm going to turn that bill over to Frayne," he said. Frayne was his lawyer. "He'll get some results."

She looked off into a blue-and-green landscape framed by the door. "They've always been nice to Laura . . ." she said. "Kathy has loved her since the first grade." He said nothing.

"Laura's been exposed to a lot through Kathy," she went on. "She's stayed in their home, and they've taken her places. She's learned things."

He turned to look at her. "Are you telling me we have to *pay* for his daughter's friendship?"

She seemed not to hear. "And whatever he is, his wife's a real lady," she said.

"She is. That's a fact. Like you," he said.

She met his eyes directly. "You have to be born that kind of a lady," she said.

A band of sunlight, teeming with dust motes, fell across the center aisle. Frowning, he stared at the dust motes. Silence seemed to build up in his ears like pressure. The ticking of the clock grew louder. He noticed the time.

"What's holding up Willie?" he burst out. "He's been gone thirty minutes! We ought to send him last, instead of first!"

Saturday was the biggest day of the week in the store. Martha got up at daylight and put on a pair of flat black shoes she called "old-lady comforts." The day before, trucks had brought in produce, dairy products, bread, and a supply of soft drinks. Their fresh meat was limited to chicken and pork chops, with less perishable wieners, bologna, sausage, and bacon. Hamburger, fish, pot pies, pizzas, and TV dinners were kept frozen. All day Friday, Martha and Willie had helped put up what the trucks had brought in, cleaning and straightening as they went.

Though it was still payday, Tom knew it had become more Martha's and Willie's day than his. He farmed with machinery now. The bigger and better his machines, the fewer men he needed. Once it had taken him most of the day to pay the help. Now he could do it in no time.

He was still the boss, however, and still there. He too got up early and put on clean clothes, the khaki-colored pants and shirts worn by middle-class farmers too old or too conservative for jeans. Small farmers, who did their own work, wore overalls. Tom's outfits were the same seven days a week, but he saved the newest and best for Saturday and Sunday. On Sunday, and for trips to town, he put on a tie. When Laura was a child she said he looked funny in a suit, and he knew what she meant.

He suspected that most customers would rather be waited on by Martha or Willie, that they hoped he would be back in his office or out on the place. He waited on them anyway. There were also a few, black and white, who preferred him, asked for him, waited until he was free before coming forward with their lists. For them he did his best, then waved aside the bag boy hired for Saturdays and carried out the bags himself.

Today was as busy as ever. By ten o'clock Martha's wavy hair, pulled back and pinned up, had lost its early-morning neatness. Full-breasted and feminine, she looked more like a mother in the kitchen than the manager of a store. Willie's face glistened and his eyes were intent.

Helping his mechanic, Bud Howell, pick out a ventilated cap with a visor, Tom glanced up to see a black man in white coveralls hand a sheet of paper across the counter to Martha.

The man was called Pig and lived in town. He cooked for a living, and had a reputation for making the best barbecue, Brunswick stew, and gumbo in the county. People booked him months in advance for barbecues and fish fries. They took him on vacations and trips to the coast. Everyone knew him.

"Excuse me a minute, Bud," Tom said. "I have to help my wife."

At Martha's side, he smiled cordially. "How you, Pig?" he said. "You down to cook for Mr. Jeff?"

"Yes, sir, That's right." Bowing slightly, Pig smiled back. "He sont you his list."

On a yellow legal sheet, everything was listed in large quantity: hard cabbages for slaw, bread and butter (good oleo, if no butter), mayonnaise, Tabasco sauce, cases of Cokes, big bottles of ginger ale and club soda, tea bags and sugar, potato chips, sweet mixed pickles, lemons, vinegar, black pepper. Paper plates (best quality), big paper cups, dinner-sized napkins.

Tom's heart seemed to rise up in protest. Except for the meat and liquor, Jeff's whole barbecue was in his hand. He reread the items, calculating as he went, then turned toward the office.

"I'll be right back, Pig," he said.

Martha gave him an anxious, warning look. People were waiting, so she couldn't follow.

In the office he went straight to the ticket file and back to the A's. Jeff's total, in Martha's careful figures, was even more than he had thought.

He placed a sheet of stationery on the stand-up desk and wrote, "Can't fill order until account is paid." Immediately he could see Martha's face, worried and vulnerable, loath to give offense for any reason. He knew what she would say. After staring briefly at the paper, he added: "In full, or substantial amount."

He attached his note to Jeff's list, folded both pages, and sealed them in an envelope.

"We can't get to Mr. Jeff's order right now, Pig," he said, handing him the envelope. "Give him this for me, will you?"

It was a while before Martha could talk to him.

"What did you do with that order?" she said, accusing not asking.

"What do you *think* I did with it?" he asked.

She looked at him and said nothing.

"Did you read it? Christ A'mighty! You want me to pay for a party you ain't even invited to?"

"But I didn't care. It was just—"

"What made you bring it up, then?" he flung at her, but her face was so bleak he wished he hadn't said it. "Don't worry. I'd have done it anyway. If I ever foot the bill for something like that, it won't be for a bunch of high-flyers better off than I am!"

"Always money . . ." she said.

"Damn right." As he turned away, he remembered something. "Did anybody help Bud find a cap?"

"I did," she said. "We found one."

"I went off and completely forgot him," he said.

Jeff and the barbecue were soon crowded out of mind, but Tom did not enjoy the rest of the morning. A vague sense of depression stayed with him. At noon he wasn't as hungry as usual. The iced tea tasted strong and bitter. There was too much salt pork in the vegetables, and too much cornstarch in the pie. He was sure the rutabagas, which he liked, would give him indigestion.

When he went back to relieve Martha, she was busy filling an order. Willie was out front selling gas. With a toothpick still in his mouth, Tom went to get fishhooks for two black boys who kept staring at his eyes.

The fishhooks were on the other side of the store, in the bottom of a showcase where he had to squat down to get them. When he stood up, Jeff's wife, Katherine, was already in the store, heading toward Martha.

Jeff was in and out of the store each week, charging, borrowing, killing time. His wife was never with him. If she came to the camp house more than once or twice a year, no one saw her.

Now as she hurried toward Martha, both of whose hands were full of Campbell's soups, Katherine Arrington was clearly upset. Tall and slender, in old slacks and a shirt, she had obviously rushed off without taking time to fix up. Even so, she had class, Tom thought.

"Mrs. Moore?" In the hush around her, Katherine's voice, high and urgent, could be heard throughout the store. "Oh, Mrs. Moore! I need to speak to your husband!"

Tom had left the black boys and fishhooks.

"Right here, Mrs. Arrington," he said, walking up beside her. "Let's step back to my office."

Country people, seated around the fireplace and standing in the aisle, stopped talking to look and listen. Grape and orange drinks, small cakes, and candy bars were forgotten in their hands.

Closing the door behind them, Tom took a seat on the stool. Too late he remembered he wasn't supposed to sit when a woman was standing. Getting up now would look worse, he decided, and stayed where he was.

From a worn leather bag on a shoulder strap, Jeff's wife took a handful of bills, unpaid, that Martha had sent months ago. As she held them out, her face was so flushed it looked swollen.

"I didn't know about this, Mr. Moore," she said. "I'm sorry. My husband—"

"Miss Katherine—please!" He lowered his voice to a near-whisper. "There's no hard feelings. It's just business."

"But it's not right! You look after your business and pay your bills."

"I come up the hard way," he said. "It was a case of have-to with me."

"You were better off, believe me."

Her hand was trembling as she opened a checkbook, to write out a check for the full amount.

"I appreciate your coming, Miss Katherine." His voice suddenly rasped, like a scratched phonograph record. He stood up and pushed the stool aside. "Now let's forget the whole thing—my wife will fill your order."

"Jeff took it on to town, Mr. Moore," she said. "But thank you, just the same."

On the way out she stopped to say good-bye to Martha, who looked as if she had a sudden fever, and to say that Kathy had heard from Laura not long ago.

When they finally closed the doors to the store, night had fallen. Quickly and efficiently, with few words, they emptied the cash register, locked the safe, and turned out the lights.

Outside, everyone had gone. The moon was new. There were few stars, and the sky seemed higher than usual. Their footsteps, loud on the hard dry ground, died without echoes.

With a flashlight, Tom led the way to the modest bungalow he had built conveniently near the store. Martha held the light while he opened the door.

At the flip of a switch the living room appeared, like a window display in a small-town furniture store. The sofa and chairs had been ordered sight unseen from a wholesale catalogue. Larger in scale than expected, they made the small room look crowded. Over the mantel a mirror, flanked by candlesticks without candles, reflected nothing but the opposite wall. Except for lamps, ashtrays, and framed pictures of Laura, the tables were bare.

Without a word, Martha went to the bedroom to take off her "old-lady comforts." She never talked much on Saturday night, so Tom did not consider her silence tonight unfriendly.

He did think she would ask what had happened in the office; but all she said before turning out the light was, "We forgot to feed the cats."

"They're supposed to catch rats," he said. "That's their business."

He was sure she had seen Katherine Arrington's check with the others.

The next day, as on every other Sunday, they slept later than usual, then went to Sunday School and church. Both were from generations of Baptists, but they attended the community church, which was Methodist.

Afterward Martha heated up a dinner the cook had prepared the day before, and washed the dishes. She seemed to enjoy working in the kitchen on Sunday. The cook was dirty, she said, and Tom had a hard time getting her to stop scrubbing pots, pans, and surfaces. He did not help in the kitchen.

In the afternoon they read the paper and rode around the farm to look at the crops. As they rode, he outlined plans for the week ahead. Farming was one way to separate the men from the boys, he said. A few more days without rain, and the soybeans wouldn't have a chance this year.

"We'll get a rain," she said. "Don't worry. My corns hurt."

When they came back to sit on the porch and relax, the last thing in their Sunday routine, cars soon began to go by as if randomly spaced, one after the other.

"Oh." Tom sat up in his chair. "On their way to the barbecue. Wasn't that Judge Hixon?"

"I don't know." Martha got up. "I need to water the flowers."

"Somebody can do that in the morning," he said, but he knew she would go and not come back.

He sat alone and watched each car go by. Many people saw him and waved, since he was well known in the county. Some were busy talking and did not look to one side or the other, but everyone seemed to be happy and enjoying life. In the mild weather, windows were down and fragments of laughter flew out like discarded wrappings. The cars were all late models, clean and shining as in a parade.

When the last one had gone, Tom did not look with

pride, as on other Sundays, at his store or the land he owned in all directions. Taking a small, black-handled knife from his pocket, he opened a blade and began to trim and scrape his nails.

If someone had only had his eyes fixed, he thought, the rest wouldn't bother him the way it did Martha. He could get along without barbecues and pedigrees, even education, the worst drawback of all. But he did hate his eyes. As always in low moments, he saw them as they must look to the world—ugly and pathetic.

Hours later, when the cars came back, he and Martha were asleep. Martha did not wake up, and he didn't know why he should have. There was no loud laughter or honking horns such as sometimes disturbed them in the middle of the night—just cars going by in the darkness.

Unable to go back to sleep, he turned from one side to the other. His restlessness finally woke Martha.

"What's wrong?" she asked, with a hint of irritation, her words muffled by the pillow. For the day ahead of her, sleep was important. "Why don't you take an aspirin?"

After that he tried to lie still. But it was almost dawn before the blackboard of his mind, filled from one end to the other with questions he couldn't even understand, much less answer, was erased at last by sleep.

D I S T U R B E R
O F   T H E   P E A C E

In the bathtub of her upstairs World War II apartment, Jeanette soaped herself compulsively. At this moment Frank was at home or somewhere else with his new wife (wife!), while she was here trying to wash off the past half-hour with Dr. Wells. It did not seem possible.

"Please call me Jim," Dr. Wells had once said humbly in the darkness, but she couldn't. He was her doctor. He was also twenty years older and married. She had hardly known him until her wedding to Frank was called off and she went to him sick. Before that he was only the young doctor who took care of people in Martindale when the old one couldn't. She didn't call him anything, just "you."

Tonight he'd come early on his way home from the hospital, but it was never the same. Her phone might ring at six A.M. or ten P.M., whenever he could manage to misappropriate the time.

"Jeanette?" he would say from an empty office, lab, or booth somewhere. "Could I come over?"

She would begin a slow intake of breath, meant to become an incorruptible no.

"Just to talk?" he would put in quickly, before it could happen.

He always came, but not just to talk. It was as if he brought chocolates, and without wanting candy but desperately wanting something, she would eat nuts, nougats, creams, soothed at the time but sorry later. She brought up their problem again tonight.

"This has got to stop," she said. "Your wife, or somebody, will catch on any minute. It will be the talk of the town."

"Forget my wife. I've told you all about that."

"But there are your children."

He sighed deeply.

"And what about me?"

"You?" He shook his head. "I'd like to straighten it all out and try to make you happy, Jeanette. But you won't give me a chance. You won't let go of Frank."

"Well, I'm *trying* to let go."

Her eyes filled with tears. She was always quick to tears when he was there. He held her fraternally while she cried and waited with patience until she was through. The rest was like eating the chocolates.

Looking down at her body, pink from the heat of the water, she was disgusted. She had gained nineteen pounds. At first, unable to eat at all, she became so thin her suffering was visible and the whole town suffered with her. Then she began to enjoy milk shakes, later barbecue sandwiches, and food became a solace. After that she ate and ate.

"You look fine. It's becoming," her customers said loyally. They all knew Frank had gone off to a CPA meeting in New Orleans and had fallen in love with somebody else. The wedding invitations were hurriedly canceled.

> *Mrs. James McNeil Martin*
> *Announces that the marriage of her daughter*
> *Jeanette McNeil*
> *to*
> *Mr. Robert Francis Wilson*
> *Will not take place*

Jeanette had given up her teaching job in Atlanta, so she went to work at Langley's, just for the summer. It was now the night before Easter and she was still there, selling clothes, doing windows, learning to buy. She knew she should get out of town and go back to teaching, but something had happened. She could no longer sleep at night. Unpredictable crying spells came upon her. Headaches and nausea put her to bed for whole days at the time.

She'd overheard her mother on the phone. "I don't know what is to become of her. It has broken her heart." Sometimes, instead of "heart," she said "spirit." "It has broken her spirit."

Jeanette put on a nightgown and took her nightly pills, the antidepressant and tranquilizer prescribed by Dr. Wells. In the lavatory mirror her eyes looked frightened ("anxious," he said). Dark half-moons sank into the plump cheeks below. Her face, still pretty, was sad even when she smiled, restless in repose. Only her hair, blond and healthy, seemed unchanged by months of grief.

The apartment, improvised from two large bedrooms in an old high-ceilinged residence, consisted of a living room and a bedroom, kitchenette and bath. The living room was too large, the bedroom small and narrow. An oblong double window, placed so high up no one had ever bothered to put up shades or curtains, faced the bed. A faded valence had been left at the top by some former renter.

Jeanette turned out all except a reading light, got into bed, and picked up the evening paper.

She would not go with her family to church tomorrow. She no longer went to church, said prayers, or felt there was anyone to pray to. Where had God been when Frank was in the French Quarter of New Orleans, falling in love with an "executive secretary"? She would join the family after church, for dinner at her mother's. Her sister, Nancy, would be there with her husband, George, and their two little girls, from Auburn.

She read until the print blurred, then turned out the light.

Something was instantly wrong. Light was still there. She lay in a flood of brightness, held in shape by the windows, as if a huge outside spotlight were fixed on her bed.

She propped up on an elbow, then sat up. What on

earth was this light? Not moonlight. Nothing she could think of or imagine.

She went to the windows.

"Oh!" she whispered. "Oh, no!"

A cross, at least five feet tall, had been put up on the Methodist Church, across the street and on the corner. It was defined by rows of burning light bulbs that lit up the darkness and brought to life the church and street below. It was positioned not at the top of the steeple but at its square base, where a bell used to be. Its rays seemed obliquely aimed at her windows.

She put on a robe, hurried down the creaky stairs, and out onto the sidewalk. This avenue was next to the heart of town, where the few houses that remained belonged to elderly widows who refused to sell, kept the downstairs for themselves, and rented out the rest. Her own landlady was in a nursing home—the reason Jim Wells could come and go. Office buildings had been put up next to the houses. Muted night lights were on in several offices. Otherwise everyone's light was out, the avenue deserted.

She stared up in disbelief. The cross was no temporary Easter fixture. It looked as permanent as the signs downtown—Langley Bros., Martindale Drugs, The Korner Kafé.

A surge of protest rose within her. This was too much. This was not fair. She did not deserve to be singled out with a cross.

The truth was, fate had set her up for what had developed. She wouldn't even know Dr. Wells, much less be involved with him, if Frank hadn't left her practically at the altar. And Jim Wells was the loneliest person she knew. "You go your way and I'll go mine," his wife had told him, years ago. Going to him for help had been like walking into a trap.

No. She did not deserve the lighted cross. And how could she sleep with it shining in her face?

Sleepless nights had sent her to the so-called clinic in the first place, and when the old doctor happened to be on vacation, an obvious trick of fate. So it was Dr. Wells who had listened to her heart, looked into her eyes with a light, and tapped her knees with a hammer. Finally he had asked if something was troubling her. She had hesitated. Then, modestly clutching the sheet to her chin, she had sat up on the examination table and told the whole story.

"It started in high school," she said, at the end. "So he was my whole life. Past, present, future."

Across the cell-like room, he had sat and listened. He wore no white coat, only a nondescript suit and tie. His hairline was starting to draw back from a face that was seldom exposed to the sun, since he worked all day seven days a week. His glasses needed pushing up on his nose. Behind them, his eyes seemed familiar with pain.

"I think I can help you," he had said at last, beginning to write prescriptions on a pad. "I want to see you again in a week. But if you need me in the meantime, just call. Day or night."

Jeanette had phoned her mother. He was the best doctor she'd ever been to, she said.

Upstairs, she decided to spend the night on the living-room couch, where the cross couldn't reach her. As she took a pillow from her bed, however, the town clock began to strike eleven and the cross vanished. When it did not reappear, she went to look out the windows. It was off, out. Could it be for the night? Convinced that it was, she took an emergency sleeping pill and got into bed.

It was midmorning when she came to, partially, regretfully. Her first thoughts were still always of Frank. Spring itself was Frank in a short-sleeved shirt. She thought of him standing behind the family at her father's funeral. Introducing her as "my fiancee." She went over evenings in Atlanta, weekends at Gulf Shores, late cold suppers in the kitchen at home.

Today he was displaced by the cross. In her mind's eye it glowed as at night. Its afterimage seemed to send out rays. It filled her whole consciousness so that her self, cowed and reduced, could not find a comfortable place in relation. She pictured her small self bowed down at the foot, then off to one side. Neither place seemed right. The cross was asking something of her, but even in imagination she could not see herself pick it up to carry. It was disproportionately large, for one thing, and also attached to the steeple. Did it want a corpus? She had been through that already, months ago. Was there more?

She got up and went to the windows. Still there, no dream. Though the lights were out, it would light up again tonight, she supposed.

She went to the kitchen, made a cup of instant coffee, and looked out to the fair Easter day. Tender yellow-green leaves had unfurled on the trees. Redbud was in bloom against a sapphire sky. Lower down she saw flowering quince, blooming jonquils, and a purple blur of hyacinths. Birds were singing, mating, carrying straw for nests.

On Easters past Frank had sent her corsages, which she pinned on new dresses before going off to church— always his church, not hers.

Frank was a Methodist. His family had been Methodist for generations. In Martindale everyone went to church except intellectuals, alcoholics, and a few eccentrics. But Frank was a dedicated churchgoer, Sunday School teacher, youngest of the deacons. He would soon rival his father with a record length of service. He had even gone to the youth group in his teens.

"Every time they open the door, *he's* there," Nancy liked to say. She had never cared for him. "The Calculator," she began to call him, when he went into accounting. "Where's the old Calculator tonight?"

Jeanette had no new dress today or even an old one that fit. In a let-out skirt and blouse, she arrived at her mother's as they drove in from church.

"Aunt Net! Aunt Net!" The little girls ran to meet her in smocked Easter dresses. They had baskets filled with paper grass, dyed eggs, and foil-wrapped candy. Each had a stuffed rabbit with hard pink eyes.

"Go outside with the girls, Sister," Nancy said, when Jeanette began to help in the kitchen. She was now exempted from all banal duties. Everyone tried to make her happy, in ways however small.

But when she told them about the cross, right after the blessing, they were more amused than concerned.

"We can get the Klan to come burn it," George said. His blue eyes glittered.

Jeanette did not smile. "I thought I'd call the mayor tomorrow," she said.

"The mayor has nothing to do with it," Nancy said, with a touch of impatience. She had taken off her Sunday dress and put on jeans. She looked younger than Jeanette, who was three years her junior.

"Who *does* have something to do with it, then?" Jeanette asked. "It's disturbing the peace. My peace."

"Nobody can do anything, now that it's up there, Sister," Nancy said. "It's just a freak thing, like an accident. You can't take it seriously. It's too tacky."

"Get some shades, pull them down, and forget it," George said. Since the death of his father-in-law, his weight in the family had increased. He liked advising the women.

"Yes," Nancy agreed. "There's nothing to do but ignore it."

"But you all don't understand. . . ." Jeanette's voice gave way. The fork in her hand shook. "I can't *stand* the cross!"

All their eyes focused on her, those of the little girls curious and wide. She looked at their faces, then put down the telltale fork, and began folding her napkin.

From the head of the table Mrs. Martin, who had been listening, rushed in as though dashing water on a blaze. "I'll call up their preacher," she said. "What's his name? Warren? He's a good man. He'll do something. Finish your dinner, Jeanette."

While the others cleaned up, Jeanette hid and hunted eggs with the children, but their laughter and cries of surprise seemed remote. She had come to be in a different reality from that of her normal, happy relatives, and even from her former self. And over her reality, hardly endurable before, now loomed a cross—garish and artificial, but still a cross.

She left early, to lie down and rest before it came back on, she told her family. Like flags at half-mast, they stood in the front yard and watched her drive away.

The phone was ringing when she unlocked her door. "I talked to Mr. Warren," her mother said. "The cross is a memorial to the James family. It comes on at twilight and goes off at eleven. He doesn't think he can do anything about it, but he wants to come and see you, talk to you."

"No, Mama. Not that. I can't see him."

"Well, I'll get the shades tomorrow. And you come back here tonight. I'm expecting you." Her mother's desperation sounded close to her own.

Mechanically she made up her bed and straightened the bedroom. She had had no contact with Frank since the morning after his trip to New Orleans. She had been living at her mother's house, the wedding only three weeks away.

She had already known something was wrong. He did not call from New Orleans. When she tried to get him at his hotel, he was always out and did not respond to her messages. On the last day, he called to say he would be home that night and see her at nine in the morning.

The minute she opened the front door and saw his face, she stepped outside and closed the door.

"Let's sit out here," she said. Her mother's porch was private and pleasant, its furniture warm from the heat of the sun. On the arm of the chair she sat in, Jeanette's hand found a soft bubble of paint. She ran her finger over and over it, careful not to mash it.

Later she couldn't remember his words, only their content. He couldn't go through with the wedding. It wouldn't be fair to *her*. He hadn't known what love was before he went to New Orleans. He was sorry. . . .

"Are you sure?" she had asked. Her heart was pounding so loud she was afraid he could hear it. She thought of her wedding dress in its plastic cover, safe in the guest-room closet. "Don't you want to wait and be certain?"

That would only make it harder, he had said. There was no need to wait.

Two months later he brought his bride home to Martindale. Since everyone put up a wall around her, Jeanette hadn't seen him face-to-face. His wife hadn't come into Langley's as she'd feared.

Now it would soon be twilight and the cross would light up. At first, like the moon before sundown, it would hardly be noticeable; but the darker the night became, the brighter the cross would shine. It would take over her bedroom until almost midnight. Night after night.

She knew she couldn't stand it. No use to try. As in a nightmare or a trance, she went to the phone on her bedside table. She sat down on the bed, picked up the phone book, and looked up the new number. With a finger that felt inanimate except for its tremor, she dialed. Frank said hello with the disinterest of a doctor or lawyer after hours.

"Frank, this is Jeanette," she said, with effort.

"Oh." He was instantly on guard. "How are you?"

"Well, I have a problem." Unable to control the vibrato in her voice, she spoke as rapidly as possible. "Your church has put up a cross that shines in my win-

dows at night. Shines in my face, actually." She rested as
from great exertion. "I haven't been well lately. I have
trouble sleeping, and all."

"I'm sorry to hear that." He sounded more polite
than sorry.

"I don't think I can stand that cross in my face every
night. I'm really nervous. . . . You're a Methodist," she
said, with sudden force. "I thought maybe you could do
something."

There was a moment of silence. "I don't have anything to do with the cross," he said. "What made you
think I did?"

She paused. Hadn't she just told him?

"Why don't you pull down the shades?" he asked
quickly.

"It's not that simple," she said. "This apartment isn't
air-conditioned and I need the air."

"Well, what did you think I could do?" Distance did
not conceal the edge on his voice.

"I didn't know. I thought maybe . . . You couldn't get
them to turn it off, could you?" Even as she asked, she
knew the futility of the question. "Maybe they could turn
it on just for special occasions, like Easter and Christmas, or revivals."

"That's ridiculous," he said.

"Do you think your father could do something?" she
persisted, against all her instincts.

"Daddy? He doesn't have any more to do with it than
I do. Besides, it would be just as embarrassing for him as
for me."

"Embarrassing?"

"Well, yes. You ought to understand that. Look, you

sound out of control. You need to call up the preacher or somebody, not me. There's just nothing I can do about the cross. Besides, it doesn't bother anybody else. Everybody else seems to like it."

She could think of nothing more to say but continued to wait.

"I'm sorry," he said, washing his hands of it. If her feelings were hurt, she had brought it on herself, the tone of his voice implied.

She eased the receiver back on the hook, took her hand away, and laid it in her lap.

Down the street a dog began to bark. Someone's back door slammed. Through the quiet late afternoon a woman called out, "Pat-see?" After a short wait a child answered reluctantly, "Ma'am?"

Outside Jeanette's windows, cars began pulling up to the curb. Car doors slammed. Voices of young people rose up, laughing, talking, calling out to one another, boys and girls of the youth group. They hurried into the back of the church, where doors closed behind them. Presently they were singing an Easter hymn. "Alleluia!" they sang, spacing out the syllables over several bars. The music reached Jeanette as from a radio station not quite tuned in.

Inside her room darkness came sooner than out, where daylight lingered. As it faded, light from the cross seemed to materialize, gather strength, and focus upon her. She no longer tried to escape. Like an animal picked out of darkness by the hunter's light, she stared into the heart of it, mesmerized and blind.

GOOD-BYE, CLIFF

With a small foot in a neat black oxford, Miss Emma pushed the front-porch swing back and forth. She meant to go ahead and decide about the tombstone now, this afternoon, so she could forget it. Cliff's grave had been on her conscience long enough.

First she looked about her. It was spring, and the big water oaks towering over her small house were all leafed out. Beneath their huge limbs her front yard, so shady no grass would grow there, was clean of rock or feather, the ground still striped and swirled by the licks of her brush broom. A brick-trimmed walk, bordered with thrift, ran straight to the road. Redbud and dogwood bloomed in the woods beyond and a faint scent of flowering crab apple clung to the air.

Miss Emma was outwardly thin and frail, but her eyes might have belonged to a veteran of some long, major war. Through gold-rimmed glasses she examined the swing, settee, and porch chairs on which she had put new coats of paint last week. The cushion covers were all freshly washed and ironed. Her potted ferns, lined against the wall, were dark, healthy, and bristling with fronds.

Satisfied with everything in sight, she brought her attention back to the tombstone. Just before Easter, she and her oldest son, Elam, had gone to clean up the family lot in Mount Zion cemetery, where she was reminded again that everyone had a marker except Cliff. Even unnamed babies, whose dates of birth and death were the same, had little headstones that said "Infant," son or daughter of someone, while all her husband had was a cape jasmine bush she had rooted from a cutting. So she finally wrote the tombstone man, who had come yesterday and left a book with pictures and prices.

"I guess I'll try to do something about your daddy's grave," she had said to Elam, coming back from Mount Zion. They had gone in his car, with the hoes, rakes, and yard broom sticking out of a lowered back window.

But Elam made no comment, not a word. He had no intention of helping with a tombstone, and neither did the other three. Cliff had been hard, too hard, on his boys, whipping them like animals until they were big enough or strong enough to hold his arms so he couldn't.

So she didn't blame them. She didn't even blame herself until the past few years, when the debts were paid off and a little money was put aside. Oh, the debts! Cliff had died unexpectedly, without warning, just lying down to take a nap as usual while she washed the dishes. And all he had left them was the debts. Fifteen years it took her to pay them all, with a double mortgage on the little red-clay farm and no help but young boys. Nobody thought she could do it at the time, she found out later. Everyone said it was impossible.

But she went to work the day after the funeral and never let up until she paid every cent. Each time she took a trip to the bank, she took the boys with her, one at a time. And she let them carry the payments, even Bobby, the youngest.

"Give him your money, son," she would say, sitting in the banker's office, in front of the big, polished desk. "And get the receipt."

The banker would look at Elam or Sam, Hoyt or Bobby. "So you help your mother farm, do you?" he would ask.

"Yes, sir," they would answer.

"Well, you're a fine young man," the banker would say, getting up to shake hands. "Good luck to you all."

She had wanted the boys to know what they were doing and why, so they could hold up their heads in spite of patched hand-me-down clothes and half-soled shoes.

A mourning dove began to call in the distance, "Oooh, coo, coo, coo." The sky was so clear Miss Emma almost expected to see right through, into heaven itself. Having reached the age of sixty-five, she thought about heaven and the hereafter more often than before, though she never seemed to get beyond the gates of pearl. She simply could not imagine a city of gold, garnished with jewels. What stubbornly came to mind instead was a kind of Sunday afternoon peace, in a place of shimmery light without walls or buildings, and without fatigue, loneliness, or worries over money. She found herself looking forward to it, in a way.

Her sons wouldn't talk about the tombstone, but they were always bringing up a subject that she didn't care to talk about either. They didn't think she should stay on out here alone, without transportation or a telephone, seeing no one but the postman for days at a time.

"Did you see Miss Livvy or Mr. Ben last week?" one or the other was sure to ask every Sunday.

Livvy and Ben were her nearest neighbors, out of sight and a mile down the road. Livvy used to walk over to see her at least twice a week, and she went there in between. Now Livvy's blood pressure was up and she seldom came, while she herself was tired by noon and didn't feel like walking. Sometimes Ben brought Livvy in the truck after supper, but he didn't like to drive at night because of his eyesight.

"No, I didn't see them," she had to tell the boys, more and more Sundays. "Not this week."

"Come on home with us, Mama," Elam begged. "You know we built that room on especially for you, and it's just sitting there empty."

All the boys seemed to want her, and even their wives insisted, though she wondered how the wives would take it if she did agree to go.

"I'll come before long," she always promised.

"You'll come when it's feet first," Bobby, her baby, predicted.

He was probably right. When she left here, she

wanted it to be for her heavenly home. The place grew harder to keep up and more lonely all the time, especially in winter. And she was anxious to see her mother and father again, her sister Maude, and the rest.

Would she see Cliff again, too? she wondered.

Cliff would be there all right, she felt sure. He'd been a member of the church and he went every Sunday, sometimes with whiskey still on his breath. No matter how he cursed and ranted during the week, beat the boys, or lay drunk on his bed while they did the work, he got up on Sunday, shaved, dressed, and drove the pickup to Mount Zion. In the cab, the two of them rode in silence while the boys sat behind, on the sides of the truck bed, huddled against the cab for protection from the wind. The minute Cliff walked into church, carrying his Bible, he was like a different person.

He could be in heaven without being in the part where she would be, Miss Emma thought. It would be so much bigger than anyone could imagine, to hold all the souls gone on through the ages. Besides, in a spiritual body, she might not even know Cliff. There would be no actual marriage there, she knew. The Bible was clear on that. They would all be like the angels in heaven, according to Saint Mark.

With a sigh she opened the book in her lap and began to turn the pages. The tombstones in front, big blocks or flat slabs of marble, were for the rich, she knew, not for people like her; but she looked at them all, turning slowly. The style she saw most often, page after page, was one big headstone for husband and wife. That would be cheaper in the long run and easy on the children. There would be nothing for them to do when she passed on except have a little marker put at her feet. But it made her think of a double bed somehow and, frowning, she began to turn more quickly. When she came to a section of small, single markers near the back, she stopped and began to study each picture in detail.

Looking up to rest her eyes and think, she checked the road out of habit. Whatever came her way, came on that road. Now, barely in sight, she saw a moving object, whether animal or human, large or small, she couldn't tell. Her glasses needed changing (another expense she would soon have to face), so she watched with interest as the object grew larger and more distinct.

It was Miss Livvy, walking fast with her head down, arms churning back and forth like the wheels of an engine.

Livvy's too fat to walk like that, Miss Emma thought. Closing the book, she laid it beside her in the swing. When Miss Livvy came nearer, she got up and went to the top of the steps. "Where's the fire?" she called out, in a voice full of welcome.

Miss Livvy looked up beneath the brim of her sun hat, but she said nothing in return. Lifting one hand in a kind of promissory wave, she hurried doggedly on.

Long before she came up the steps, Miss Emma knew something was wrong. She had watched Miss Livvy come down the road and up the walk for years, bringing jars of preserves, pieces of cake, cuttings of plants, help in times of trouble. She was the friend of a lifetime, as close as family, as dear as a sister. Today her hands were empty.

"Sit down, Livvy," she said, offering a rocker pulled up and turned to face the swing.

Miss Livvy's face was a damp, rosy red. In the soft depths of her combined throat and chin, a pulse beat strongly. Her clean print dress was limp with perspiration. Falling heavily into the chair, she dropped her sun hat on the floor.

"Want a drink of water?" Miss Emma asked.

"No, I thank you," Miss Livvy said shortly.

Miss Emma sat back in the swing and waited. Patience was a virtue the hard years had taught her, submission to delays, reverses, changes of weather, the passage of time. She watched the redness fade from Miss Livvy's face, the wet hair loosen from her forehead. The sheen of moisture began to evaporate from her plump arms and hands.

"What's wrong, Livvy?" she asked at last.

Miss Livvy began to rock back and forth nervously. Her bosom rose and fell. "Emma, you know I'm no busybody," she said abruptly.

"Busybody?" Miss Emma didn't understand.

"But I've come to tell you something."

Now it was Miss Emma's turn to be nervous. She could think of nothing about which she ought to be "told." Still, everything inside her seemed to tighten up. Could one of the boys be in trouble?

"What are you talking about, Livvy?" she asked.

"I'm talking about that tombstone you intend to buy for Cliff."

"Why, Livvy!" Miss Emma gave a tight little chuckle. "You had me worried. What about the tombstone?"

"Elam told Ben what you're about to do," she said. "Spend your good money on that . . . that . . . devil!"

Miss Emma looked down at her hands coarsened by

years of drudgery, the joints of the fingers all enlarged.
She had never talked about Cliff to anyone, not to a soul.
So how did Livvy know?

"Ah, well." She examined her bare left hand. The
wedding band had worn so thin it came apart, years ago.
It was in an empty spool box in the top drawer of her
dresser. "I just want to do what's right, Livvy. He was the
boys' daddy."

"What's right!" Miss Livvy said. "If it was you dead
and Cliff living, you'd do well to get a fruit jar full of
flowers out of somebody's yard, and you know it."

"I don't plan to buy the most expensive kind," Miss
Emma said. "Just a plain marker for his name and such.
It's only decent."

Miss Livvy's brown eyes refused to agree. "Well, I
can't stand the thought of it," she said, like a covered pot
about to boil over. "I'll not sit by and do nothing."

Miss Emma felt something coming, something she
wished she could hold back or stop, but she didn't know
how. Her heart seemed to wake up as from sleep.

"Emma, do you remember those Averys that lived in
town so long, there by the gin?" Miss Livvy asked.
"Trashy people? The yard full of old broken-down cars?"

"Why, yes."

"You recall that oldest girl?"

"The one with black curly hair, and big . . .?" Miss
Emma cupped the air at a great distance from her own
flat chest.

Miss Livvy nodded. "That was Cliff's woman," she
said.

The swing no longer moved back and forth. There
was no sound except, high in a tree, a sudden distur-

bance among the birds. After much chattering there was a quick exit of wings, then a return of silence.

"Maybe it was just talk," Miss Emma said at last.

But Miss Livvy shook her head. Her eyes had filled with tears. "Everybody knew it but you," she said.

Miss Livvy's words seemed to sink like stones, to disappear without a ripple. But Miss Emma had heard. "How did everybody know, Livvy?" she finally asked.

"His horse was tied in her yard half the time, and she talked it everywhere. *Bragged* how much he spent on her."

Miss Emma stiffened as from a blow.

"That boy of hers was just like him," Miss Livvy went on. "His spit image."

"I never saw him," said Miss Emma, relieved over one thing. Her own boys favored Cliff very little. They were more like her own side of the family.

"No, you never saw anything," Miss Livvy was saying. "You were at home, trying to make a living."

In the swing, which would have held three her size, Miss Emma sat holding on to a metal chain hooked to the ceiling. She watched Miss Livvy lean over to wipe her eyes on the turned-back hem of her dress.

"Don't cry, Livvy," she said, as though Miss Livvy were the injured one, not she. "After all this time, it don't make much difference."

Miss Livvy looked up. "Well, I hope it makes enough to stop you from buying him a monument!"

Like an old memory book, the past suddenly opened up for Miss Emma, falling apart to a picture of Cliff all dressed to go to town. He wore clean clothes, his shirt still warm from the heat of her iron, and he looked the way he always looked when he left for town, hurried, excited, his eyes shifty. That look had always puzzled Miss Emma, and now she understood. What a fool she had been all those years, she thought, with a rush of shame. How innocent and blind!

"You don't blame me for telling it, do you, Emma?" Miss Livvy said. "I stayed awake half the night, worrying about it."

"No, Livvy." Miss Emma's voice wavered. "I *thank* you. I wish you'd told me years ago!"

"I'd have done the same for a sister," Miss Livvy said.

"I know that."

Their eyes met, warm brown and sober gray, now misted over, and held as in a handclasp.

Two cats, one yellow and one gray-striped, and an aging liver-spotted bird dog had appeared. The cats came to rub against Miss Emma's ankles, while the dog turned round and round, then lay down on the walk to keep an eye on her. They were hungry and waiting to be fed.

Miss Livvy noticed. "If you're upset, Emma, I'll stay on. Ben said he'd come for me if I'm not back by sundown. But if you're all right, I ought to start home."

"I'm all right, Livvy." Miss Emma stood up. "You go ahead."

She stood at the end of the walk and watched Miss Livvy go, and then she just stood there. It was time to gather eggs and put up the chickens, but she did not start the chores at once as on every other afternoon of her life. Instead she went back to sit in the swing, remembering. She couldn't stop going back for things to explain themselves, like that look on Cliff's face when he left for town.

Years of ginning seasons came back like dreams, with herself and the boys picking cotton alone in the blistering sun, and Cliff gone on the wagon until late at night or the early hours of morning. Drugged with fatigue, she would sleep and wake, sleep and wake, listening for the sound of wagon wheels, or the trace chains' rattle.

"They all got ahead of me," Cliff would say in the gray, hopeless dawns.

And the next day, handing her the money, "The bale wasn't as heavy as you thought."

How much had he given away? Miss Emma wondered, with a deep inner ache. Ah, God, the toil it took to make it, and the things they did without! The boys wore shirts she made at night by lamplight, patches all her pains couldn't hide, shoes with pasteboard cut and fitted inside the worn-out soles. They had been cold, hungry, sick without a doctor. When home remedies failed to work, Hoyt's eardrums had ruptured. Bobby failed a year in school because he couldn't see the blackboard. Sam still limped from want of attention. And all the time their own father!

Her face burned as from an open oven when she remembered a certain far-off night. Less tired than usual, she had moved close to Cliff on the mattress.

"Go to sleep," he'd said, turning his back coldly. "You're too bony for me."

Was it going on then? she wondered. Bobby had just begun to walk, she recalled, and it was her last pregnancy.

But what was the point in torturing herself? What was the sense in remembering? Cliff had been even worse than she thought, and that was the end of it, the only difference between knowing and not knowing.

Now she knew he'd been more than lazy, cruel, and a drunkard. He'd been a thief, who stole from his own wife and children. And not only thief, but liar, adulterer, hypocrite . . .

She caught her breath in horror. Cliff had died without warning. He'd had no time to repent!

Miss Emma sat frozen, hardly breathing, as before the visible descent of a naked, cast-out soul. Cliff wouldn't be in heaven at all.

A small, unconscious sigh of relief escaped her. The afternoon had chilled and faded, but still she didn't get up and start the chores. The chickens went to roost and the cats disappeared. She didn't move but sat staring out upon the rosy horizon, overcome with awe before a new and frightening aspect of the universe. Even in the realm of right and wrong, where the eye couldn't see, all was in order, like the seasons, the tides, the stars in their courses.

The lowing of a neglected cow brought her back to the present and the tombstone, as to a memory already mellowed by time. In her mind's eye Cliff's marker was in place already, a parting gesture, a last farewell. How had it ever troubled her, she wondered, a passing sacrifice here on earth? Beyond, in mystic clarity, lay endless vistas of shimmering peace.

TONGUES OF FLAME

The Reverend Zack Benefield, evangelist, had been called in to Rehoboth Church like a doctor to a patient. Rehoboth was more than a hundred years old and, some thought, dying. A country church, surrounded by large farms that had swallowed up the small ones, many of its members had moved away. A few were attending churches in town, but the majority had simply lost interest and, more often than not, stayed home on Sunday morning.

Tonight, the third night of a week-long revival, Rehoboth held more people than it had in twenty years.

Benefield's sermon was over. His doubleknit coat hung on the back of the pulpit chair. In spite of two fans directed on him, his short-sleeved shirt clung wetly to his skin. His broad face was flushed and his eyes seemed to send out charged blue rays. He had left the pulpit to come down near the congregation.

"Before I came out here," he said, "I looked up the word *revival* in my son's new college dictionary. Just out of curiosity. What it said was, 'to return to consciousness, to life.' Now." He lowered his head, then raised it. "If you really want a new life, for yourselves and this old church, I want you to stand up and be counted tonight. I want you to come down here and give me your hand. Because if you don't want that, I just as well pack up my suitcase and head on back home."

In the third row from the front, Dovey Goodwin sat listening, her hands in her lap. A farm wife, middle-aged and overweight, with a sweet face and brown eyes, she was one of the few who kept Rehoboth going. On her left was her husband, Floyd, and next to Floyd, E. L. Nichols, in church for the third time in anyone's memory.

Floyd sat slumped in the pew, his thin legs crossed at the crotch, watching Benefield as he would watch a bird in a tree.

E.L. had begun to shift his weight from one side to the other, and to change the position of his hands and feet. From time to time he stifled a cough. He was a farm overseer and spent his days in the sun, yet his skin never tanned but stayed tender and red as if inflamed. When drunk, his color sank to a clammy white, from which it rose like a thermometer as he sobered up.

Benefield called out a hymn number and raised both arms, on which thick, wheat-colored hair sprang up golden in the light.

"While we sing now, won't you come?"

From behind him, to the left, came a piano introduction full of bold off-notes. Abigail Wright, whose forebears had founded and named Rehoboth, was the white-haired pianist. Bringing an evangelist to Rehoboth had been her idea. He was a guest in her home. Never married, since no suitor had been good enough for her parents, she lived alone in the homeplace, its cedar-lined lane within sight of the church.

Benefield unleashed a powerful baritone to get the song under way, and people began to fill the aisles coming forward.

Dovey squeezed past Floyd and E.L. Yes, she wanted a new life for Rehoboth. What would she do if its doors ever closed? She had come to this church for as long as she could remember, and even before, in the arms of her mother. She had in turn brought babies of her own. Her people were buried in the graveyard behind it. Sunday and Rehoboth were one and the same to her.

She was also here on Saturdays, dusting and cleaning, usually alone. Depending on the weather, Floyd took a nap in the truck or came back to get her. Now and then other women helped wax floors or wash windows. Miss Abby gave money, fixed flowers, and fed the preacher with the help of a cook, but she did not clean up the church. "Dovey is our housekeeper," she said.

"God bless you, sister." Benefield clasped her hand, looked her in the eye, and turned to the next in line. "Thank you. God bless you."

Half the congregation was already at the front. Others followed, one at a time. Floyd stayed behind with E.L.

On the last verse Benefield lifted a hand to Miss Abby, who stopped playing. "Anyone else?" He checked the pews like an auctioneer. "Will you come?"

E.L. lowered his head, covered his mouth with his hand, and coughed. When singing resumed, Floyd kept his eyes on the songbook and sang in a drone like a faraway tractor.

Afterward, as they turned to leave, hands reached out in all directions to touch E.L. on the arm, pat him on the shoulder.

"Glad to have you, boy."

"See you tomorrow night."

Miss Abby hurried through the crowd. "I wouldn't take anything for you being here, E.L.," she said.

E.L. had worked for her family most of his life, first for her father, then for her brothers, who farmed the family land but made their homes in town. "Drunk or sober, he's the best farmer around," everyone said.

Benefield stood at the door shaking hands. The church was small, with a vestibule in front and Sunday School walled off in back. The rest of the building was a rectangle focused on the pulpit. Rows of pews lined the center, with shorter pews down each side. Two aisles divided the sections. There was a smell of old wood and musty songbooks and, over all, an aura of quiet. When empty of people, the sound of dirt daubers building nests went on all day.

Over the vestibule rose a modest steeple in which hung an iron bell, the end of its rope just above the heads of the people. The bell, once rung each Sunday morning, had been silent so long it was no longer missed.

There was no light in the churchyard except from

windows of the building, and the sudden blinding headlights of departing cars and trucks. Behind it the adjoin-
ing cemetery lay in darkness. From time to time a pair of
headlights picked out several tombstones, to flash them
like a preview onto the screen of night.

People lingered in shadowy groups near the steps.
When Benefield had clasped the last hand and let it go,
he took out a handkerchief and mopped off his face,
neck, and arms. Then he came down the steps like a
winning athlete. Smiling and joking, but still on the job,
he made his way to where E.L. stood with Floyd and
Dovey. Without looking at E.L., he spoke from the side.

"You're on my heart, brother. I'm praying for you."

When E.L. drove off, everyone turned to the
Goodwins.

"Three nights in a row!" someone said. "How did you
do it?"

Floyd looked at Dovey.

"All I did was feed him a time or two," she said.

The patent-leather purse on Miss Abby's arm flirted
with light from the vestibule. "My hat's off to you, Dove,"
she said. "He never let me feed him."

On the way home, Floyd and Dovey met no other
cars. Rabbits ran across the road in front of them. The
eyes of small animals glowed from the woods and the
roadside ditches. The air dried Dovey's hair, damp
around the edges.

"I hope they don't scare E.L. off," she said. "Carrying
on so much."

"Shoot, he might like it," said Floyd.

It had all begun in the spring. All winter, after work,
E.L. had been passing out in his parked truck, some-

times in the middle of the road. On the way home one night Floyd, who worked on a neighboring farm, decided to bring him home and try to sober him up.

Dovey had helped willingly.

"He hasn't got a soul in the world," she would say, as she made hot coffee and warmed up food night after night.

The Goodwin children, grown, married, all in different places, called home regularly. When they realized how often E.L. was there, being sobered up and looked after by their parents, they didn't approve. Gertrude, the oldest, finally spoke for the rest.

"You don't have enough to do since you got rid of us, Mama."

"Now, that's not so," Dovey had protested. "But E.L. is just so pathetic."

"Well, don't get the idea you and Daddy can straighten him out, after all this time. He's got psychological problems, with all that drinking and stuttering and being a loner all his life. He needs more help than you can give him."

"What do they expect us to do, let him *die?*" Dovey asked Floyd later, telling him what Trudy had said. "Besides, he hasn't been drunk in a month."

"He ain't quit, though, Dove. By no means. You know that."

"But he's just drinking beer now. You said so yourself."

What Floyd did for E.L. he did without faith, Dovey thought. Floyd was a good man and would help anybody. What she did was different. She could see E.L. sober and happy like other people. He could have a good life if he only stopped drinking.

Once or twice she'd seen him dressed up. In a suit, with his pink skin, prematurely white hair, and pale blue eyes, he didn't look like other farmers. There was an air of refinement about him, especially in his manners. He was careful about ashes, for instance. If she forgot to give him an ashtray, he caught ashes in his cupped hand or, if he thought no one was looking, dropped them into the pocket of his shirt. Though he smoked all the time, one cigarette after another, he'd never once dropped ashes on her floor.

She liked to watch him eat. Floyd took her cooking for granted, but E.L. seemed to enjoy every bite. After a meal he folded his napkin exactly as it had been before, no matter how long it took. The way his hands shook, it was touching, like the efforts of a child.

"A f-f-fine meal," he would say. "M-m-mighty good. Everything."

The night after Trudy's call, Floyd had to stop and move E.L.'s pickup before he could get by on the road; but he didn't bring E.L. home as before. Instead, he took him to the overseer's own house and put him to bed.

The first thing Dovey said was, "*Why?*" Then right away, "We'll have to go down there after supper."

E.L.'s house was white with a tin roof, and a yard full of bird dogs barking all together when they drove up. The only company he has, Dovey thought.

On the porch, a single straight chair had been turned over and propped against the wall to protect it from the rain. The front room was furnished in what E.L. called "Mama's things." A picture of his mother in late middle age hung on the wall. There was a painting of a stag at dawn, antlers high, eyes straight ahead, and a bookcase filled with books.

Everything needed dusting. In his own house E.L. paid no attention to ashes, Dovey noticed. There were ashes on the arm of his mother's sofa and on her hand-hooked rug. The kitchen sink was full of dirty dishes. An empty pork-and-beans can, with a teaspoon still in it, sat on the kitchen table.

E.L. lay in a stupor in the bedroom, where Floyd pulled up a chair to watch TV. Dovey cleaned up the kitchen, then brought scrambled eggs and bacon to the bed.

"E.L.," she said firmly. "Wake up."

Floyd had turned around to watch. "You better let sleeping dogs lie," he said.

"He's got to have something in his stomach," she said. "He'll go right back to sleep."

On the way home, Floyd kept yawning. He'd been up since four-thirty in the morning. "Trudy may be right," he said. "We can't do nothing with E.L."

"Well, if we can't, maybe the Lord can," Dovey said shortly.

She'd been up even longer than he had, since she had cooked his breakfast. "Miss Abby says there's to be a big revival at Rehoboth. Maybe we can get him to go."

When the time came, it had been easy.

"Revival starts tomorrow night, E.L.," she said on Saturday. Come eat supper and go with us."

"O-k-k-kay," he said. "What time?"

But when they had eaten and started to go, he had balked unexpectedly. "I'll c-c-come on behind you," he said. "Y'all might want to s-s-stay a while, and I got to get up in the m-m-m—"

"Morning." She said it for him, and he seemed to be relieved.

So now he'd been there sober every night. Dovey held the thought with deep satisfaction as they drove into their yard. In the kitchen they stopped to drink water. A geranium, framed by ruffled curtains, bloomed in the window. It was canning season and jars of freshly canned tomatoes were ready to be put away on the pantry shelves.

"You know, E.L. is listening to that preacher," she said, as she poured ice water into glasses.

"Yeah." Floyd smiled. "Old Zack puts on a good show, him and Miss Abby."

"I'm not talking about any *show*, Floyd." She opened the refrigerator door. "Want a piece of pie?"

"Might as well." He took his place at the kitchen table and waited to be served.

She got out a lemon icebox pie, two plates, and a knife. Knife in hand, she paused to look at Floyd.

"I believe in miracles, myself," she said.

He took the perfect piece of pie she handed him. "I don't know why," he said. "You sure ain't never saw one."

Since childhood Dovey had knelt by her bed at night, to pray before getting in it. Except in times of trouble, she went quickly over the names of her friends and loved ones, prayed for the sick and needy, asked daily strength and guidance for herself. She prayed for sunshine or rain for the crops. If she stayed on her knees overlong, Floyd knew something was wrong and moved to the far side of the bed. Tonight she prayed somewhat longer than usual, for E.L. and his soul, Floyd suspected. He moved on over, just in case.

During the night Dovey had a dream. E.L. was in bed with them, and she was in the middle. Floyd slept soundly, but she was awake and aware that E.L. was too.

She wished E.L. would move closer, and he did. When he put his arm around her and began to fondle her breast, she was flooded with pleasure.

She awoke shocked and ashamed. Why would she dream a thing like that? She hoped to forget it when she went back to sleep, but it popped up in her mind the first thing next morning. She turned off the alarm on the clock and got out of bed. She didn't know where dreams came from, but they came in the darkness of night and should stay there. Now it was almost daylight. In the kitchen, since there was time, she decided to make pancakes.

That night the Reverend Benefield wore a suit he hadn't worn before. The tooth marks of a comb still showed wetly in his hair. As people came in and found seats, he sat in the pulpit chair reading from a small New Testament. From time to time he raised his head and stared at the ceiling, or sat with his eyes closed in meditation. He did not look at the audience.

On the pulpit, someone had put a vase of zinnias beside the large gilt-edged Bible given by Miss Abby's family. A pitcher of ice water and a glass were ready on a tray. The collection plate was in place on a small side table. The plate was of dark polished wood with a wide brim for handling and a removable pad of worn red velvet in the bottom.

In the rapidly filling pews, people sat quietly or spoke in whispers. To make more room, Floyd and E.L. sat like half-folded shirts, arms out of the way and knees close together. Dovey didn't know where all the people came from. Over against one wall, she recognized a girl who rode the school bus with her years ago. The girl, now a woman, looked old and worn out already.

As the last arrivals tiptoed in to sit on the front row or in folding chairs in the back (all other places were taken), Benefield glanced at his wristwatch. Without haste, he took his place behind the pulpit. All movement ceased. The faces before him were like sunflowers fixed on the sun. The only sound was that of oscillating fans.

"Shall we come to the Lord in prayer?" he said.

Every head bowed and most eyes closed, but his prayer was short and spare, a quick formality before getting down to business.

"God's Holy Spirit is here tonight, my friends," he said. "I never felt it more strongly in my ministry."

He shut the big Bible and laid his hand on the cover. "So I'm going to forget about the sermon I prepared for you. I'm going to talk about something else entirely. I'm going to go where the Spirit leads me."

He left the pulpit and came around to stand in front of it.

"Just look at this congregation!" he exulted. "Isn't this something? If half you people came to Rehoboth every Sunday, you wouldn't be sending for me." He raised an eyebrow. "I'd be sending for you!"

Laughter sprinkled the pews.

"Do you know *why* you're not here every Sunday?" He waited a moment. "I'll tell you why! Because we all have crutches to keep us going, from one day to the next, one week to the next. Your crutch is whatever you use to keep from falling down before the throne of grace and saying, 'Lord, I can't make it on my own. I can't stand up to all the trials, temptations, and disappointments of this life. You've got to help me. *You* take over!"

Words began to pour out. His voice began to vibrate, then soar. It rose to the ceiling and resounded, amplified. It plummeted to a whisper and rose again, stronger than ever. He threw back his head and reached up for handfuls of heaven, looked down into a flaming abyss. He took off his coat and flung it on the chair.

When a baby began to cry, people glared at the mother until she got up and took it out. No one noticed when she came back to stand in the vestibule and listen, jiggling the baby to keep it quiet.

Spent at last, Benefield filled a glass with water and drank it off. He wiped his face with a handkerchief.

"We will stand and sing 'Revive Us Again,' " he announced. "We all know it. Let's sing it from the heart—all four verses, please."

Halfway through the song, he got down on one knee by the pulpit. Until the song was over, he prayed alone, eyes tightly shut.

"Now then." He was back on his feet. "I'm going to ask for something I've never asked for before. Not money." He pushed back the idea with his hand.

"I know that some of you good people, like people everywhere else today, lean on drugs to keep going. Tranquilizers, sedatives, pills. You have to have help and you go to the doctor. He writes out a prescription.

"Some of you rely on alcohol." His eyes moved slowly over the congregation without coming to rest on a face. "Do you know how many alcoholics we've got in America today? So many we have to have not only AA for them, but Al-Anon for the people who live with them.

"I'm sure a few of you fine young people, living in this good, wholesome environment, will try marijuana if you haven't already. We smoke cigarettes. We eat too much, *buy* too much, just to keep ourselves pacified. Temporarily. The Scripture says, 'My God shall supply all your

need according to His riches in glory by Christ Jesus.'
Philippians 4:19."

"Amen," a man's voice called out from the back row.
"Now, my friends, we're going to sing an old gospel
song, 'Leaning on the Everlasting Arms.' That's what we
need today, the arms of God Almighty! That's what our
fathers and forefathers leaned on. They never heard of a
tranquilizer, and they crossed the wilderness in covered
wagons.

"As we sing, we'll pass the collection plate. I'm
asking you *not* to put money in it. Not this time. But if
you've got a crutch with you, and if it will go in that plate,
I want you to put it there. I want you to throw away,
tonight, everything that keeps you from the saving grace
of our Lord and Savior, Jesus Christ!"

Miss Abby found the number, opened her hymn book
and propped it with care. Before she began to play, she
took a bottle of pills from her purse and set it on the
piano.

Dovey had no pills and neither did Floyd, but several
bottles were in the plate when it reached them. There
was also a package of cigarettes, to which E.L. added his
own.

As the plate moved back, collections rattled in all
the way. Down front again, it was piled so high a package
of cigarettes fell off and had to be picked up from the
floor. Besides prescription drugs, there were over-the-
counter pain relievers, antacids, stimulants, cough sup-
pressants, antihistamines.

Dovey glanced at E.L. Hunched over, he gripped the
edge of the pew with both hands. The knuckles of his
fingers were white.

"I don't think the law is here tonight," Benefield

joked, "in case we got a joint or two!"

Several of the young people laughed, then glanced around guiltily to see if anyone had noticed. Everyone looked at the plate, then at Benefield.

"I know some of you will regret giving up your crutches," he said. "They cost money for one thing. I also know if you get home and can't sleep without your pill, you might not come back tomorrow night! So I'm asking you, when the service is over, to come down and take back whatever belongs to you. We did this to make you think, my friends. When you get home tonight I want you to think, and to pray for God's help as you've never prayed before."

After the closing prayer, people didn't look at each other directly, as usual. Everyone was reluctant to go down for his crutch, so someone picked up the plate and began handing it around. Those hunting through it looked sheepish.

When Dovey turned toward E.L., he had gone.

"Brother Benefield went too far this time," she said to Floyd, in the car heading home.

"He's an evangelist, Dove," Floyd said. "They're supposed to stir people up. They're all red-hot."

"But did you look at E.L.?"

"Yeah. He was nervous."

"That's what I mean. And he slipped off without a word about tomorrow night, or anything. I didn't even tell him to come on to supper."

"He wouldn't go back for his cigarettes and didn't have no smoke. That's why he took off so quick."

At home they drank water in silence. Having been up four nights in a row, they were tired. Dovey's prayer, instead of being longer, was shorter.

But once in bed, she couldn't sleep. This would be the turning point for E.L., she thought. Brother Benefield had preached straight at him. She kept bringing her thoughts back from pictures of E.L. passed out in his truck or his unmade bed, sick of Rehoboth, and sick of her for ever getting him there. At the same time, she could plainly see him sober, in a clean blue shirt, sitting beside her and Floyd with every pew in the church filled, as tonight.

"Help him, Lord," she prayed. "Now it's up to you."

Asleep at last, she dreamt the church bell was ringing, and when she woke up, it was. She held her breath and waited to be sure, then shook Floyd.

Floyd reached for his pants. In the country, a church bell ringing in the night is a call for help in emergency. While she slipped on her housecoat, he unlocked the door.

"Something's on fire!" He was already down the steps, calling back to her. "Get the buckets while I turn the truck around."

"It's Miss Abby's house or the church," he said, starting off before she could slam the door to the cab. They sat up straight, trying to see ahead, as he drove fifty miles an hour down the dirt road.

Tongues of flame, in billowing smoke, leapt into the dark sky before them. The flames were red-gold and glowing, with sparks shooting off in the night like fireworks. All around was a reddish haze and, in the air, a malignant crackle.

"Lord God," Floyd said, when the blaze came in sight. "It's the church!"

Dovey opened her mouth to speak, but no sound came out. She forgot to close it as she looked at Rehoboth, flames coming out of the roof.

Cars, trucks, and people in nightclothes were everywhere, but the fire department from town was already there and in charge. Up close, most of the flames were confined to one wall. A fire hose, snaked in through the vestibule, was trained on the bottom of the blaze. There was a loud rushing of water and hissing of steam. People stood watching with small flames in their eyes.

Brother Benefield had been the first to see it, someone said. He was also the one who called the fire department and rang the bell.

The wet pulpit, with the Bible still on it, had been brought out into the churchyard. Pews sat haphazardly about. Songbooks, Sunday School books, and Bible pictures for children were scattered on the grass. Off to one side, someone was lying on the ground beneath a tree. Two men were standing nearby, as if on guard. Floyd looked at the man on the ground.

"How did it start?" he asked suspiciously.

Dovey felt her heart stop, then lurch forward.

"Oh, E.L. Nichols was in there drunk." The voice that answered was filled with disgust. "Smoking, they think. Miss Abby kept hollering, 'Get the Bible, save the Bible.' That's the only way they found him. He could have died from the smoke."

"That bottle was still in his hand, though." There was a short, bitter laugh.

Dovey took hold of Floyd's arm. When he went to look at E.L., she went too, holding on.

In the smoky orange light, E.L. lay on his back, his head turned to one side. He no longer wore a shirt. Over his undershirt, the coat to his suit spread beneath him like failed wings. One pants leg was up above his sock. From time to time a hand twitched, or a foot. Once he halfway opened his eyes, then groaned and shut them.

As the flames were drowned, people began to move around, talking, laughing, asking questions.

"How did they ever stop it?" someone asked. "It was all heart pine."

"Why, the hand of God was in it, that's all."

A practical voice spoke up. "They had it insured, didn't they?"

Dovey held to Floyd's arm and said nothing. For a time he seemed not to notice, then turned to look at her. "You ain't about to pass out too, are you?" he asked. "I got to go speak to the preacher."

She let his arm go, but walked close behind him.

"I'll take E.L. on home, Reverend," Floyd volunteered.

"Brother, that would help," Benefield said, and added a thought of his own. "If you could bring me back here, I'd follow in his truck and get it out of the way."

Dovey climbed into the cab. She did not watch as they lifted E.L. into the bed of their truck. She paid no attention to the preacher behind them, his headlights politely dimmed.

Floyd drove slowly, easing over bumps and washouts. "Well, I guess that takes care of the revival," he said.

She looked at the road and said nothing.

At E.L.'s house, Floyd and Benefield lifted E.L. from the truck bed and, draping his arms around their necks, carried him up the steps to his door. Dogs barked at their heels all the way.

"Shut your mouth!" Floyd finally burst out at the one beside his leg.

While she waited in the truck, Dovey saw without interest that trees and bushes were all still black, but the sky had turned a gun-metal gray. It was almost morning.

Floyd and Benefield came out and closed the door behind them. They got in the truck, one on each side of Dovey. Doors slammed. The preacher adjusted his bathrobe and the legs of his pajamas. The cab was crowded, so he eased his right shoulder out the open window. No one spoke as they headed back to Rehoboth.

Benefield shook his head. "I've been accused of preaching hell and brimstone all my life," he said. "But that's the first time I ever set a church afire."

When the meaning sank in, Floyd guffawed. He couldn't stop laughing. He set off Benefield, and they laughed together.

"Yes, sir," Floyd said, when he stopped to catch his breath. "You outpreached yourself that time!"

They laughed again. The crisis was over. They had done what they could, and nothing was ruined except the wall of a church.

Dovey did not join in the laughter. She saw nothing funny in anything, anywhere. Staring before her in the gray, breaking dawn, she felt she had never been through such a night in her life. Her mind still blazed out of control, and there was no one to put it out for her. Not Floyd. Not the preacher. No one.

THE AMARYLLIS

It came to be the first thing he thought of each morning. What did it do overnight?

He would get up and go straight to the parlor for a quick look. More fascinated each day, he would hurry through breakfast, then take his second cup of coffee back to sit and study the newest development.

The amaryllis was now two feet tall, its first lilylike bloom the diameter of a salad plate and a twin bloom rapidly opening to the same glowing red. There was also a slightly lower second stalk with three heavy buds still to come.

The whole thing was so beautiful it had come to dominate the entire house. It was not only alive but dramatically alive. It had presence, almost like a person, and he was conscious of it off and on all day. More and more, however, it seemed to be asking something of him, he wasn't sure what.

Today, Thursday, with the bloom at its peak and the bud half open, he got the message. He couldn't have something that special in the house and not share it. But with whom? The question had flawed every good thing that happened since Margaret died.

Margaret would have loved the amaryllis, but all the other appreciators he could think of were either busy working, far away, or dead.

Their son, Angus, was as worthy as Margaret, in his way, but he was both busy and far away. Still, the thought of Angus with the flower was irresistible. At seven-fifteen he dialed the house. Mary Ann answered.

"Oh, Judge Manderville?" She was surprised, also anxious.

"Nothing is wrong," he assured her. He never called in the morning except in an emergency. "I wanted to invite you all down for the weekend. I have something to show you."

"*This* weekend?" Silence. "Angus has already gone, Judge Manderville. He has surgery this morning. But I know we can't come. We're all involved, the children too. What do you have to show?"

"Remember the amaryllis bulb you gave me? It's blooming and it's unbelievable."

She laughed. "I know. It's a hybrid from California. Did I tell you?"

"Yes. But you didn't prepare me for anything like this. Maybe I couldn't have been prepared. It's the most beautiful thing I ever saw."

"I'm glad you like it, Judge Manderville. Angus will be too. I'm really sorry we can't come. It'll be a while, two or three weeks, before we can get away, I expect. You know how things are here."

He knew. He could see Mary Ann dressed for a nonstop day, about to chauffeur his grandchildren to school, her time all planned straight through to dinner.

"Well, thanks, Mary Ann." He knew she had to go. "Sorry you can't make it. Love to everyone. Good-bye."

Going back for his coffee, now cold, he entered the parlor with a sense of apology, and left at once without looking at the flower. He hadn't really expected that they could come, so why was he disappointed?

His son had become almost inaccessible, he thought, as he washed up the dishes. He knew Angus was there but he no longer saw him except on holidays, parts of vacations, and when he was pressured into going for annual physicals. Angus belonged to his patients first and his immediate family second. The Judge no longer thought of himself as immediate.

Which was not really fair. Angus didn't like the distance between them. Sometimes he called as late as ten, apologized, and talked on. One night the Judge was awakened at ten-thirty to hear Angus saying, "I just called to say I miss you, Dad. Go on back to sleep." Angus' voice had sounded bone-tired and lonely, and the old father-sonship had flamed up to bring the Judge instantly awake and available. They had talked for an hour.

There was no doubt that Angus loved him. To Mary Ann he thought he must be something of an obligation, regularly and necessarily on the list but never quite convenient, certainly never a first choice. He felt she was fond of him and would visit him with reasonable regularity in the nursing home. She would see that he had a nurse, but she herself would not sit and hold his hand if the last days drew out.

His two grandchildren were beloved, close strangers. And the fact remained. He was quite alone in the world.

Hanging up the dish towel, he went to finish dressing. He could invite McGowin over to see the amaryllis. McGowin would look and never really see it. Then he would stay all day and talk about the past. "Listen, James, do you remember . . ." he would say, and launch into some long-ago episode. The Judge hadn't mentioned the amaryllis to McGowin.

In his study he tried to get down to work, as he liked to call the self-appointed task of going through the letters, papers, scrapbooks, diaries, and financial records collected in the house since the time of his parents.

"What do you do with yourself these days, Judge Manderville?" people asked him in the grocery store or on the street.

"Right now I'm cleaning out the attic," he would say, and smile.

After all those years on the bench, years of power and some prestige as circuit judge, it embarrassed him a little to say what he was busy with now, going through his and Margaret's letters and papers, trying to separate the wheat from the chaff.

On the desk before him now were several small memorandum books to be filed away or discarded. Margaret had been a reader who looked up words she didn't know, then wrote word and meaning in a small notebook. It was a habit like brushing her hair, to which he had paid no real attention.

Opening the first notebook, he saw she'd written *deciduous, synecdoche,* and *ankh,* with meanings. Then she wrote *ubi sunt,* but gave no meaning. Why not? he wondered. What did it mean? Out of context, he had no idea.

Near at hand, the phone rang. In the large, empty house the telephone was his link with the outside world, with the living. He always picked up expectantly on the first or second ring.

"Good morning, James," said McGowin.

"Hello, Mack."

"What you doing?"

"Working. How about you?"

"Not working." McGowin chuckled. "It's my birthday."

"How about that! How many?"

"You don't know? I'm eight months ahead of you. Don't you remember I got to go to school a year before you did? But you skipped the fourth grade and caught up in the fifth."

"Congratulations, Mack. Happy birthday. Are your children coming down or anything?"

"No. But they called, and I got presents from everybody. Shirts, ties, pajamas. You know."

The Judge hesitated briefly. "What're you doing this afternoon?"

"Nothing. Why?"

"What about my coming over around four?"

"Fine! Sure, James. That'll be great. I'll brew us some Sanka."

"How do you feel on your birthday?"

"I feel like hell. I know I'm on the shelf for good and I can't get used to it. Can you?"

"No, I can't either."

"We retired too soon. We should have hung on longer. But I had that little stroke. And you wanted to take care of Margaret."

"Yes. I don't regret it."

"Well. Like Satchel Paige said, 'Don't never look back. Something might be gainin' on you.' " They both laughed. "I'll let you get back to work, James. See you later."

"Have a good day, Mack."

Feeling selfish and justified at the same time, he put the receiver back on the hook. If he'd asked McGowin over, it would have started something that would go on for the life of the amaryllis. For McGowin it would be merely an excuse for companionship.

Protecting himself, however, did nothing for the plant. Sitting up there in absolute silence, it projected pressure through the walls.

He stared out the study window, trying again to come up with appreciators. All still busy, far away, dead. He sighed and gave up.

For McGowin's birthday, he decided to call the bakery and get a cake to take over. A cake with candles to go with their decaffeinated coffee.

He didn't look at the amaryllis again until after supper, when he went up and turned on all the lights in the front of the house. He turned on crystal chandeliers, table lamps, all. In his mind's eye he could see the house as it looked from the street, an 1850 colonial cottage in its original setting of trees and boxwoods, all lit up as though guests were expected.

He took a seat on the sofa, in front of which the plant stood on a low table from which he and Margaret used to serve demitasses or port after dinner. They had never cared much for society, but entertained when they had to and enjoyed having friends for dinner until her heart problems stopped even that.

In the handsome room, in artificial light, the amaryllis seemed to have taken on glamour, like a beautiful girl all dressed up for the evening. All dressed up and no place to go, he thought.

The strange thing was, he'd never "felt" anything for a plant before. On the contrary, he'd dismissed them all as more or less inanimate like potatoes and turnips, not animate in the way of cats and birds. He had bought dozen of hospital chrysanthemums, often delivering them himself in their foil wrapping and big bows, but they had seemed more artificial than real.

The amaryllis was different, entirely. He liked just being with it. Because of its size, he supposed, it seemed to have individuality, and then he had watched it grow daily, with his naked eye. Looking at the blooms, he thought of words like *pure* and *noble*, and old lines of poetry like "Euclid alone has looked on *Beauty bare.*"

In return, the plant seemed neither friendly nor unfriendly. It was simply there in all its glory, however fleeting. It was the fleetingness, he thought, that put on the pressure.

He took off his glasses, dropped them in his shirt pocket, and rubbed a hand across both eyes. Then he turned off the lights, one by one.

Next morning the second bloom was wide open, as breathtaking as the first. Red was not his favorite color, but this red was both muted and vibrant, the color of a winter sunrise, or a robin's breast. The two blooms exuded a kind of concentrated freshness like early morning in the woods, a baby's skin, or eyes just waking from sleep. Pure, unblemished by anything yet to come.

He dressed before breakfast and, while drinking coffee, wrote a note to the postman. "Eddie: Can you spare a minute to look at something in the house? Just ring the bell. Thank you. J.M." He was making a list of names when Pot arrived.

Pot came on Fridays. Years ago he had come every day of the week, including Sunday, and Margaret had taught him to clean, cook, and serve to a fine point. She had wanted him called Potiphar, a fitting name she thought, but it seemed affected no matter who said it, so they soon settled for his nickname. Pot didn't need to work now. His children were successful and had bought him a house. He drew his pennies. But he still came one day a week out of their mutual dependence, the Judge supposed.

He and Pot had been through all kinds of ups and downs together, on both sides, including the loss of their wives. They had even gone through civil rights together, with him on the bench and Pot's people in the streets. There was a time when Pot had said, "I got to stay out awhile, Judge. But you understand it ain't between me and you."

Today he met Pot at the back door. "Hurry up, I've got something to show you!"

"Morning, Judge. What you got?" Tall and lean to the bone, Pot looked the part of a king's officer, superannuated perhaps. He stood up to his years with a blend of dignity and submission. Age was becoming to him.

"Let's go to the parlor," the Judge said. At the door, he stepped aside for Pot to go first.

"It done bloomed," Pot said, smiling. "I never saw nothing like that before."

"Neither did I."

"Makes you feel like you ought to go down on your knees, don't it, Judge?"

"It does."

Pot sighed. "Well, I got to get on to the house." Bowing unconsciously, like an Anglican to the cross, he backed out of the room.

"I'm inviting some people in to see the flower," the Judge said as they went to the back hall. "Not many, maybe a dozen."

"You want to serve something?" Pot opened the closet door and got out the vacuum cleaner. He put on an attachment as carefully and precisely as if it were a saxophone.

"Coffee, maybe, if anyone wants it. But Mr. McGowin will be here for lunch, I expect."

"I'll take care of it."

A surge of love for Pot rose up in the Judge's chest, remained like a cramp as he put Eddie's note in the mailbox. How could he have overlooked Pot as an appreciator? Pot had looked at the flower with what it deserved, reverence.

He squared his shoulders and hurried to the phone with his list. If the elect couldn't come, he would get them from the highways and hedges. He put on his glasses and began to dial numbers, beginning with his nearest neighbor whom he never saw, separated as they were by three wooded acres.

He said approximately the same thing to each. "This is James Manderville. I have something here that you might like to see. It's a hybrid amaryllis in bloom, really beautiful. I hope you'll drop in if you can." Any time would be convenient, he said. He'd be at home all day.

And then he called McGowin. When it got down to bedrock, McGowin was all he had. McGowin said he'd be right over.

The rest of the day was a happening. McGowin arrived first, in a tweed coat and tie, his face red from chronically elevated pressure for which he took pills when he didn't forget them. He chose to sit on a chair opposite the amaryllis and stayed there all morning, a kind of noncirculating co-host.

When a lady entered the room, McGowin rose at once, a cross between southern gentleman and perpetual fraternity boy drilled in manners, and stood stalwartly until she sat down or left. He was fluent with anecdotes, flattery, and occasional wit, an old party man back in action.

The Buick dealer and his wife, neighbors, came around ten, the Buick dealer being his own boss, and able to take off at his pleasure. It was obvious that they were glad to be there, and to say later they had been. They did not come to see the amaryllis.

"I've seen them before, Judge," he said of the plant. "They come in other colors, too. Pink. White. Some are even variegated, but yours is beautiful.

"How old is this house, Judge? Did you inherit the antiques or collect them yourself? They're worth a fortune now. Look at those mirrors!"

His wife asked, "What kind of table is that, Judge Manderville, with the mirror below?"

It was called a "petticoat table," he explained, and why. He answered all questions and showed them the whole house. Then Pot served coffee. Their faces glowed with deference and interest. They had been here before, they told him as they left, but had never had a personal tour and they loved it. As they said, they had already seen an amaryllis.

As she started down the steps, the Buick dealer's wife looked him tentatively in the eye. "If you ever need anything, here all alone, you call us, Judge Manderville," she said. "Day or night."

"I may have to do that," he said. "And I won't forget. Thank you."

"I see your light at night through the trees, and I think of you often," she said. "Your wife was lovely."

Suddenly, to his great surprise, his eyes filled with tears and so, he saw, did hers.

The flower-shop owner, in the midst of making floral arrangements for a funeral, had to squeeze in her visit just before lunch. She wore a knit pantsuit, another squeeze, the Judge thought; she might as well have been stark naked. He caught a glimpse of McGowin's eyes. Poor old devil. He'd been a real ladies' man in his day and still got occasional calls from widows. But he no longer rose to the bait. After his wife died and the little divorcée turned him down, he seemed satisfied with, even somehow proud of, his bachelorhood.

The flower-shop owner was all business, however. "Do you know how much the bulbs cost, Judge? I'd like to get a few for the shop if they're not too expensive."

He said he'd get the address from Mary Ann and she could write the nursery. She sat long enough to drink a quick cup of coffee and smoke a cigarette.

"People pick the worst times to die," she said. "They wait until I have a wedding or a big party, like now. Then they all try to go at once. And you know the old superstition, that if there's one there's got to be three? It never fails. I've seen it happen so often it scares me."

"Well, don't look at James and me," said McGowin. "We've got other plans."

At noon Pot called them in for T-bone steaks, baked potatoes, and a fine tossed salad. The Judge and Pot always ate well on Fridays, but the Judge usually did the cooking while Pot worked on the house.

"This is better than my birthday, James," McGowin said, looking around the table set with Spode and good silver.

They ate hungrily, saying little. McGowin cut his steak cleanly to the bone on both sides, eating fat and all, plus large chunks of French bread and butter.

"Bring out the rest of that cake, Pot," McGowin directed when they'd finished. "And light up the candles!"

"You brought your cake over, Mack?"

"Sure I did. I'm still celebrating, or holding my own wake, I don't know which."

With one quarter missing but with the candles lit, their small flames bowing over backward as he walked, Pot brought in the cake on a round silver tray. Ceremoniously he set it in front of McGowin and placed a cake knife beside it.

Catching the spirit, the Judge said, "Get out a bottle of cream sherry, Pot. Put it in a decanter."

Pot was smiling. Wearing the white coat he kept in the pantry for special occasions, he soon came back with a decanter of wine and two Waterford sherry glasses on a tray.

"Hot damn!" said McGowin. "Long live the big petunia—or whatever the hell its name is."

Since he drew laughter, McGowin was inspired to go on. "What do you think that thing is, Pot, male or female? It looks like a stud petunia to me, but it could be a liberated female. They outdo us every which way now, you know."

Eddie the postman rang the doorbell as if on cue. Pot went to let him in while the Judge and McGowin took their second glasses of wine to the parlor.

Eddie was a fine appreciator. Standing straight as for the national anthem, he made a ringing statement. "That is the most beautiful thing I ever saw in my life, Judge Manderville. That is really something. I wish my wife could see it."

"Bring her over, Eddie," said the Judge. "Bring her, by all means."

"Just call before you come, Eddie," said McGowin. "So James will have his shoes on."

"His shoes, Mr. McGowin? Ha Ha. You're still a card!" Eddie came a few steps nearer McGowin, leaned down and said in a whisper intended for the Judge to hear, "I've known the Judge for years, you know. He's a real gentleman. A gentleman if I ever knew one."

"Scholar, too, Eddie." McGowin winked. "Don't forget that."

"Oh, yes, sir. A scholar, too. You should see the books and papers I bring him."

Eddie said he had no time for coffee or wine, though a glass of wine would certainly be nice. People had to have their mail on time or they got upset. All down the street they were waiting for him right now, he told them.

There were no more visitors until late afternoon. McGowin's body, struggling with too much food and alcohol, both forbidden, dragged down his spirit like a stone. He first began to nod, then put his head back on the chair and slept soundly, snoring from time to time. The Judge went back to his notebooks in the study. He too felt drowsy, but down the hall he heard the vacuum cleaner going. If Pot could work, so could he.

Ubi sunt was not in the dictionary they usually used. So that was it. Margaret had been reading in bed, probably, and hadn't felt like getting up for a word. In the unabridged dictionary, which badly needed dusting, he found it at once: "adj. (L. 'where are (they)?') Relating to a type of verse which has as principal theme the transitory nature of life and beauty."

Suddenly Margaret's wordbooks became intimate, as if they were journals, in a way. Someone else would have to throw them out, he decided, not he.

He took out his handkerchief and dusted off the dictionary, then shook the handkerchief and put it back in his pocket. At his desk he pushed the wordbooks aside and sat staring out at the winter afternoon. The light of the desk lamp seemed to focus on his hands, quietly folded.

Soon after the hall clock struck four, McGowin appeared in the doorway, rumpled and dazed. "Any coffee left, James?"

"Yes. Let's have some."

They went to the kitchen, where a percolator of fresh coffee was set on "warm." At the kitchen table they drank a cup together, black, and in silence.

"Thanks, pal," said McGowin, draining his cup. "I got to be going."

"You'll miss the others."

"Can't help it, James. I'm through for the day. Has Pot gone?"

"No, but he should have finished by now. Would you give him a ride?"

"That's what I had in mind. Round him up."

McGowin drove a twelve-year-old Mercedes, but he drove it less and less, having been warned by the police about driving across yellow lines, turning into wrong lanes and onto one-way streets.

As he and Pot drove off, their faces said the party was over and they were tired. Their faces also said they'd been to many parties, that they were always over, and everyone went home.

The legal contingent arrived together after five, though not in full force. To be strictly ethical the Judge had kept his distance from other lawyers while in office. When he retired he might as well have died, he sometimes thought. Now only the district attorney and two young lawyers, with their wives, showed up. There was also the small daughter of one of the couples.

When the Judge asked the child's age, she grinned and held up four tender fingers.

The lawyers wanted drinks, not coffee, and the Judge was glad to have good Christmas scotch and expensive birthday bourbon to bring out. A happy hour was soon under way.

Both the lawyers and their wives, however, took the amaryllis in stride. Sitting around it in the parlor, one wife quickly abstracted an article she had read.

"There's a whole new thing about plants now," she

told them. "They're supposed to thrive on tender loving care. They like to have music played in the room, like to be talked to. It seems to be a proven thing. They want love and affection like everybody else. You should talk to it, Judge Manderville."

A lawyer, not her husband, interrupted. "But I also read where that talking-to business is explained. People breathe out carbon dioxide and plants breathe it in. So it's not a matter of TLC, but chemistry."

The amaryllis was dismissed. "Have you kept up with the house-trailer controversy, Judge?"

Opinions flew at him from the lawyers while their wives sat drinking, smoking, listening. The little girl sat on the floor beside her mother's chair, holding on to what appeared to be a French shopping bag filled with toys. She didn't take out the toys, however, but stared at the amaryllis. From time to time she changed her attention to a person or object in the room, but always brought it back to the flower.

The Judge noticed. After a while, he got up and moved to a chair beside the child.

"What do you think of my flower?" he whispered.

"I love it," she whispered back through a wide, tongue-cluttered smile, then ducked her head, blonde hair falling around her cheeks. From her hidden mouth she said something he couldn't hear.

"What, dear?" he asked.

Conversation had stopped and everyone was looking at the child.

She raised her head only enough to meet his eyes with her own. "I want to touch it," she said.

"Well, I think *it* would like that too." He led her to the flower and lifted her up.

"Easy now," cautioned the mother.

With one finger she reached out, gingerly touched a red petal as though it were hot, and laughed delightedly. When the Judge put her down she didn't move. "I want to kiss it!" she cried.

Everyone laughed except the mother, who said, "We're going too far now."

But the Judge lifted her up again. "Kiss it easy, then," he said.

Wrinkling her nose to avoid the long, yellow-padded stamens, she pressed one cheek lightly against a bloom. Her lips missed altogether.

Her mother stepped up to lead her away.

"No!" The child stood stubbornly, close to tears. "I *want* it. I want to take it to my home!"

"Oh, Lord, here we go." The mother gripped the child's arm with authority. "Time to leave, Judge Manderville. It's been delightful. Come to see us soon. Promise me you will!"

On the porch, as his visitors walked away, the Judge heard the phone ring. It was Angus saying Mary Ann had told him he'd called, that they would try to come in two weeks and spend one night. The Judge could tell Angus was pleased to hear about his flower show, about guests having been in the house.

He made a quick check to see that all the doors were locked, then gathered up empty cups and glasses, overflowing ashtrays. He took them all to the kitchen but left them unwashed, unemptied. Like McGowin and Pot, he was tired. Too tired even to eat, he decided.

As he undressed, however, he thought of the amaryllis alone in the parlor. In bedroom slippers, he went back and turned on a light. The flower stood as beautiful as ever. Carefully, he picked up the pot and carried it back to his bedroom, where he set it on a table in front of a window. From there he could see it first thing in the morning.

He slept soundly all night but woke up vaguely depressed. In front of the window, backed by candid morning light, the amaryllis's blooms were like heavy translucent bells. Their hue, lightest at the edges, grew deeper and darker in each secret throat. In the sunlight, the living veins were apparent as never before.

But were the blooms quite as fresh, really as perfect, as yesterday?

On the second stalk, all three buds were opening at once. Their promise, however, was not as exciting as the first. The composition of the whole plant—pot, blooms, stalks—was no longer as good, for one thing. The center of interest was being lowered and to the wrong place. He couldn't analyze the difference. He only knew that any change, or beginning of change, was already for the worse.

Each day the amaryllis continued to do something new but in a downhill direction. The first blooms passed their prime and began to age in the same way that people did, the Judge thought. There was the same pitiful withering around the edges, subtle drooping and shriveling, gradual letting go of form. The shrunken petals finally turned the color of purple veins in old legs and hung down like deflated parachutes.

The lower set of blooms was smaller than the first and seemed replicas, not originals. Petty princes, not majesty.

The Judge was vaguely ashamed that he lost interest

in the plant toward the last. When all the blooms had died, he was told to stop watering the bulb and put it away in a dark place, or even outside in the ground.

When he cleaned and straightened the house for his children's visit, he put the pot in the back-porch pantry. Tall green leaves had grown up around the stalks, and they flopped over awkwardly, hanging off the pantry shelf by the side of empty fruit jars, obsolete ice-cube trays, discarded dishes, and cooking vessels with missing tops.

He was told to leave the pot in the pantry and forget it until next year, when he could bring it out, start watering, and the amaryllis would grow and bloom again. It seemed incredible, but all the gardeners and flower people assured him it was true.

FRUIT OF
THE SEASON

The Deep South is at its best in early May, when the last
cold spell is over and the heat has not yet arrived. Leaves
and grass are still the tender green of Easter. Wild
flowers liven the countryside and, above all, the magnolia starts to bloom. Days grow long and fireflies light up
the slow-falling darkness. In early May of 1959, dewber-
ries were ripe in Alabama.

Three black children, Cato, Daisy, and Jones Lee,
had picked the first berries half red and sour, and had
eaten them on the spot. When they looked again after
days of rain, they ran home for a bucket and picked it
full, each berry a jewel of pearly dark drupelets.

Their mother, Bessie Lee, was pleased when she
came home from her cooking job. She made them a

deep-dish pie called "lally-hoo," both sweet and tart, its juice royal purple on the cracked, chipped dishes from which they ate. Bessie told the children to pick again the next day, and every day while berries lasted. In a good season there would be enough for jelly and jam, plus all the pies they could eat.

"Go all cross the pastures and 'long side the road," she told them. "Just take a good stick and watch out for snakes."

So the children left early each morning, soon after Bessie went to work for Frances Marshall, the white landowner's wife, and a row of filled jars began to grow on the kitchen shelf.

"Miss Frances want some jewberries too," Bessie told them one morning. "Y'all better pick her some today."

Picking berries had now become work, not play, for the children. They had already picked along the road, where cars passed and people waved. Today they would pick in a pasture behind their house and farther from home. They dillydallied until midmorning when Cato, who was ten and the oldest, put on a battered felt hat cut full of diamond-shaped air holes.

"Les go, y'all," he said. In one hand he carried an empty syrup bucket, in the other a stick cut and trimmed by his mother's new boyfriend's knife.

They walked single file, with Cato in front and Daisy close behind. Jones, the youngest, followed at his own pace. They had already crossed the cattle gap and were well into the pasture when Cato looked back at Jones.

"Where your stick?" he wanted to know.

Jones lowered his round, chocolate-brown head. He

wore nothing at all except knee pants held up by a strip of cloth tied diagonally, front and back, across one bare shoulder.

"He ain't got no hat on, either," said Daisy. She herself had on a ragged straw hat, long sleeves, and brown oxfords sizes too big. In one hand she carried a hickory stick like a staff.

Jones lagged behind more and more. By failing to respond, by calling no attention to himself whatsoever, he hoped his brother and sister would forget.

"Better go on back, Brother," said Daisy, up ahead.

They went on walking down a cow path, one behind the other. Yellow butterflies zigzagged around them. In the distance a mourning dove called, waited, and called again. There was no other sound except the dull clop-clopping of Daisy's big shoes.

"This pasture full of rattlesnakes," Cato said, in practiced awe-inspiring tones. With each step he tapped his stick like a cane. "Rattlesnake Pilates. Them the kind won't run. They *mean*. They 'tack you, eat you up!"

"But not if you got a stick, they won't," said Daisy.

Jones looked back. The small lichen-gray house seemed far, far away, the distance between crawling with snakes. Doggedly following, his chest began to swell up and out. His cheeks ballooned. When he burst into tears, it was with an explosive bellow. Daisy hurried back to put her arm around him.

"Hush now, be quiet," she said, patting and soothing. When she looked, the house seemed far away to her too. "We git the stick next time."

But Jones continued to bellow. His rusty sand bucket had fallen to the ground. Tears rolled down his cheeks in shining rivulets and his screams seemed to echo around the world. The children were never sure what Bessie might be able to hear or divine. If she knew, she would come and whip them in blazing fury until their faces burned and welts rose up on their legs.

Daisy hastily picked a primrose and held it in front of Jones's blind, contorted face.

"Look, Brother," she said. "Want to smell?"

His sobs began to subside. His black eyes opened and started to focus.

"Smell," Daisy coaxed.

It was an old trick but a good one. Jones offered his nose and she pushed the flower hard against it. His hand, still baby-plump, went up to check the result. When he saw the powderlike pollen, thick and yellow on his fingers, imagined it yellow on his nose, he began to laugh as hard as he had cried.

"Y'all come on now," Cato called, up ahead. "I see *berries.*"

Legs hurrying, voices tremolo from quick, jarring steps, they neared a thick mass of bushes.

"Man, oh, man!" said Cato.

"Must be a million," said Daisy.

Jones stuck out his stomach, beat it like a drum, and shrieked with delight.

Cato and Daisy set to work, and the first berries played a hollow tattoo in their empty buckets. They worked quietly and separately until the outside pickings were finished, then brought their sticks into use, mashing down the wiry, sticky bushes, pushing them this way and that so as to see and reach deeper.

Jones ate berry after berry until his tongue, teeth,

and the tan pads of his fingers were purple. Then, bored with berries, he began finding things to put in his bucket. Leaves, grass, a dead grasshopper, and live crickets.

By the time the sun reached noon, Cato and Daisy had filled their buckets. Jones's had been brought to play with, not to fill, so they set out at once for the landowner's house across the pasture.

Hot and tired, they walked in silence. Cato and Daisy leaned sideways from the weight of their buckets while Jones, beginning to whimper and complain, fell behind more and more. When it seemed he might give out altogether, Daisy went back and took him by the hand.

"We soon be there," she encouraged. "Miss Frances might give us something cool to drink. You thirsty?"

At a row of trees, with the house in sight, Cato put down his bucket. Around the straps of his overalls, his naked shoulders were beaded with sweat. He lowered himself to the ground beneath a large hackberry tree and, with a sigh of relief, stretched out full-length. Daisy and Jones found resting-places of their own nearby. Jones, breathing in hot puppylike pants, lay on his stomach with one cheek against the ground. Flat on her back, Daisy looked up at the sky through leaves.

They rested until Jones got up and began tickling their necks with blades of grass, poking them with sticks he found on the ground.

Cato stood up at last, leaves and twigs clinging to his overalls like tatters. In front of him was the house, surrounded by trees. Big, white, and shady, the house had a downstairs and upstairs, two chimneys and two porches. Inside, there were so many rooms they had to have names: living room, dining room, breakfast room, den. Their mother cleaned the rooms, cooked the noon meal, and washed the dishes. When company was there, she was so late coming home they were no longer hungry, only whiny and bad, by the time she got back. If she could, she brought leftovers wrapped in a newspaper or brown paper sack. If not, she had to make them a quick pan of corn bread or biscuits.

As he looked at the cool inviting scene, Cato thought of his own hot little house and of the blackness he would never outgrow. He thought of things the grown people said when they met in the church at night. When he turned to the bucket on the ground, his eyes seemed to darken. Without a word, he gathered up the saliva in his mouth, leaned over, and spit on the berries.

Daisy and Jones watched, first with shock, then reckless approval. Daisy glanced around to be sure no one was looking, then spit on her berries too. Jones tried in vain to gather up spittle while his mouth was stretched in a grin. Laughing now, as if playing a game, Cato and Daisy spit on the berries again and again.

Frances Marshall had gone upstairs to take a nap, but couldn't fall asleep because of a problem. She had just found out that her cook, Bessie Lee, was pregnant again, with three young children and no husband. The year before, Bessie had terminated a pregnancy by taking turpentine, which the doctor said would ruin her kidneys, maybe kill her, if she tried it again.

Now it was up to Frances to take Bessie to the health

department, get in touch with the welfare people, and find another maid or get ready to do her own work again.

At first she thought the knocking on her back door was a bird dog beating its tail on the steps. Then she realized someone was there. She was not surprised to see Cato, Daisy, and Jones. They had brought berries the year before.

"Why, hello, boys and girls," she said pleasantly. "What nice berries. Are they for sale?"

Cato shook his head, no. They all grinned.

"You brought the berries to me?" She smiled. "How nice! Come in."

She held the door open while they entered the screened back porch like shadows. Not a sound, not a word.

"Have a seat, Cato." She pointed to a bench where milk buckets had once been kept. "I'll be right back."

In the kitchen she emptied the berries, exactly two gallons. Here was a gift horse with an old, familiar mouth. If she bought the berries (which came from her pasture to begin with, after they'd picked all they wanted for themselves), she would pay the standard country price per gallon. If she accepted them as a gift, they would cost her more, for as the nice white lady for whom their mother worked, she would return their cup of goodwill in full measure and running over. She would pay not only Cato and Daisy, but the little one as well. And she would give them a treat besides, lemonade and cookies, or whatever she could find.

On the way upstairs for her purse, she glanced out the window. There was the new farmhand, coming to the pump again for water, walking as if his feet were made of lead. This time Bessie's pregnancy was his fault, she suspected. He went to secret race meetings at night, Frances's husband had told her. They all did, he said, including Bessie.

Her purse was in the bedroom, and on the bed the newspaper she'd been reading. She thought of the headlines. New bus incident in Montgomery. Increased Negro voting in the primaries. Pulitzer Prizes in journalism for coverage of school integration in Little Rock.

Downstairs she faced the large, solemn eyes of Daisy and Jones. Cato's eyes were oddly evasive.

"I can't let you all *give* me the berries this time, Cato," she said. "What are people paying for them this year?"

He shook his head that he didn't know, though she knew very well that he did. Fifty cents a gallon. This was the usual strategy. He would refuse to name a price and count on the softness of her heart instead.

But her heart beat steadily on, beat-rest, beat-rest. With a smile she handed him a crisp dollar bill and, still smiling, opened the door to let them out.

LET HIM LIVE

All he had to do was wake up. The surgeon said the tumor was encapsulated and nonmalignant. They had taken it out without bothering his brain at all, so everything would be fine when he came to. He had already moved the foot and leg that were paralyzed, and sometimes a tear rolled out of his eye as if he knew things. But still he didn't wake up, and now something had gone wrong, some bleeding, swelling, something. His condition was so bad his family, including his eighty-year-old mother, had gone up to the hospital in Birmingham.

In Wakefield, where he'd been probate judge for three terms without opposition, the first thing anyone said was, "What's the news from Carter?" Only the very young, or the old and formal, called him Judge Reese. Everyone liked and respected him, both black and white.

"I sho hope the Lord don't take him," an old black woman said, sitting on the cement curbing in front of the courthouse, eating a cinnamon roll. "Do, it won't be nobody to keep them folks straight. Everybody know Amzi and them can't run no cotehouse." Two black girls in jeans, sitting farther down, turned to look at her coldly.

Members of the churches were all praying for him. In the chapel of his own church, on the corner of Jeff Davis and Green, an around-the-clock prayer vigil was in progress. Every half hour people went in and out, taking part in an unbroken chain of petition for his life.

Down the street, Saint Thomas's Episcopal Church was without a priest and had been for months. Its members were so few, so hard to please, and so set in their ways that the bishop had trouble finding a priest to take them on, even temporarily. Among the communicants were a state legislator whose opinion had to be heard on every parish matter, a retired admiral accustomed to command, a conservative banker, and a woman liberal. Several young couples dutifully brought their children while their middle-aged counterparts, duty done, came or not as they pleased.

Of the remaining members, most were widows with gray hair and good incomes, but there was one who had to do sewing and alterations to support herself and her handicapped son, Arthur. There was a busy doctor who never came, and one dedicated Christian, a sixty-year-old woman. Between priests, two lay readers kept things going; and once a year in November, the women put on the best bazaar in town.

When Carter grew worse, Sally Wingate, president of the churchwomen, called Rich Callaway, the senior warden.

"Carter's got to live, Rich," she said. "If he dies, they'll take over the town and county both. What do you think of our having a prayer vigil too?"

"Well." Rich was the conservative banker. He stood for tradition, even in what he wore, long-sleeved shirts and ties the year round. "I never heard of us doing anything like that, but like you say . . . Who will you get to pray?"

"Oh, we'll all have to help. Everybody. And for more than just thirty minutes."

"Sounds all right to me," he said. "Where will you have it?"

"In the church. We can kneel at the altar rail, or use that prayer desk on the left. And Carter's in trouble *now*. Why don't you go on down, light the candles, and start it off? I'll have somebody relieve you as soon as I can."

Sally sat with the phone in her lap, in an upstairs bedroom of Wingate Hall. Her husband, Johnny Wingate, had died two years ago, leaving her the legacy once left to him, a house built by his ancestors' slaves. Sally was only fifty-three. In a sundress, her shoulders tanned by the country-club sun, she looked younger; and with her features, she would be good-looking twenty years from now. But there was no one in Wakefield to marry her or even take her out now and then. She was on the shelf here already, and she knew it.

She spent hours of the night worrying about her

future, but at present she was more concerned about the future of the town than she was about her own. Blacks had outnumbered whites in Wakefield for years, but by 1985 more blacks than whites voted. Led by Amzi Nettles, preaching Black Power, most blacks voted for black candidates. Already, the majority of county officials were black. Public schools were mostly black. Except for Carter, the courthouse was black. Leading businesses such as City Electric, Skinner Brothers, and Pope's Hardware had recently sold out and closed their doors, with rumors of closings to come. Whites had begun moving away from Wakefield.

Sally's dream that her son Bobby would come home to live and work had faded, but her goal was the same. She must hang on to Wingate Hall no matter what, and see that it stayed in the family if she could. Besides Bobby, she had Jane and Sarah, and there were other Wingates who could afford the house and might want it. But not if the whole town died.

After Rich, she dialed Honey Lamar, the new bazaar chairman. Short, plump, usually in high heels, Honey said she'd just served refreshments to her bridge club. She was enthusiastic about a vigil. "Why, of course I'll help. Do we have enough people?"

"If some double up, we do. I will, and I know Ann Louise will." Ann Louise was the Christian. "I'll take some of the worst time, like from one to three, or three to five in the morning."

"Two hours? Lawsy."

"Well, I'm willing. Carter's the only thing left between us and them."

"You can say that again. Something has finally

dawned on me, Sally. We should have picked our own
cotton." Honey waited while Sally laughed. "All right,
give me the list," she said, "and I'll start calling. I'll get
somebody here to help me."

Ann Louise answered the phone in bed. She had a
middle-ear problem, she told Sally, and couldn't walk
without holding on to something. Couldn't drive the car
at all. "Why can't I take my turn here at home? I've been
praying for Carter off and on all day, anyway."

"Well, somebody has to keep vigil in the church. Who
else could we get?"

"Let me think." Sally could see Ann Louise in an old
nightgown that ought to go to the Goodwill. She spent
nothing on herself anymore but gave all her money away,
and paid an accountant to help her. "What about Arthur?" she asked. "He's young. He could lose a whole
night's sleep and not miss it."

"But he's not all there, is he?"

"He's innocent, like a child, but he can pray. Better
than we can, maybe."

Arthur was at church every Sunday, prayer book in
hand, left foot dragging. He'd been injured at birth,
people said. One arm was shorter than the other and his
coordination was off, but he'd been the church sexton for
years. Except for Ann Louise, who invited him to meals,
kept him in junior books to read, and remembered his
birthday, nobody paid much attention to him. Sally
thought he'd rather not be noticed when she ran into him
dusting the church or mopping the parish house kitchen.

Honey called to say people were lined up until midnight already. Everyone wanted to help, and the "old"
widows would take all day tomorrow. She, Honey, would

take from twelve to one tonight. "That only leaves three hours after you."

"Ann Louise suggested Arthur."

"Arthur?" Honey paused. "Well, okay by me. We need to wrap this up and take a nap before we go. We won't be able to pray half asleep."

Arthur answered the phone out of breath. His mother, already scheduled for tomorrow, had called him in from mowing the lawn. "Yes, ma'am?" he gasped into the receiver.

"I wonder if you'd help with the prayer vigil, Arthur," Sally said. "We need someone for a bad time, three to five or six in the morning. You'd come after me."

"Oh, yes, ma'am. I'll come any time. Judge Reese is one of my best friends. I was praying for him anyway." He stopped to catch his breath. "He bought me my lawn mower."

At twelve-thirty Sally's alarm clock went off. She was in bed, lights out, still awake after two hours of trying to fall asleep. Glad to get up, she slipped on a skirt and blouse, combed her hair, and put on lipstick. In the kitchen she drank a cup of strong black coffee and, just before one, parked her car beside Honey's in the churchyard. The front of the church was lighted each night, but tonight someone had turned on lights in the back as well. Sally went in the back door.

Honey half knelt and half sat like a wilted plant, her forehead on the altar rail. She looked up at Sally with eyes not quite back from where they'd been the past hour.

"My turn," Sally whispered, kneeling beside her on the red velvet cushion. "Good night, love."

Saint Thomas's simple stained-glass windows were blacked out by the night, but candles burned on the altar and lights were on in the nave. Plain wooden walls, varnished when the church was built, subtly reflected the light. The altar itself, of carved walnut with a memorial plaque in front, was backed by a reredos given much later. Darker in color and slightly too wide, the reredos had caused violent objections at the time it was added, had been a source of contention for years after. Now it was considered a part of the altar. The prescribed "fair linen cloth," its embroidered IHS lined up with the cross, hung halfway to the floor on each side. The fringed brocade hangings were green.

As the sound of Honey's car died away, silence in the church became alive and tense, waiting. Sally took a deep breath and made her petition. Let him live. With everything else blocked out of mind, she began to say the words silently over and over like the Jesus prayer. Let him live, let him live.

In Wakefield, Carter walked a tightrope on which no one else could balance. Everything was now black or white, and you sided with your race or else. Carter alone could rise above it. When Amzi's mother died, before anyone knew how sick he was, Carter had gone to the funeral. And not only funeral but burial afterward, way out in the country in a black graveyard, where he stood with his hat off through the whole thing, someone said. He was the only white person there and had been criticized at the time, but not for long. Amzi's mother had been a good woman who tried to hold her wild son down, and soon everyone knew that Carter had stood there with a tumor on his brain, seeing double.

Sally thought of the Old Testament city where, if they could find one good man, the city would be spared. That's us, she thought, and Carter. She was asking for his life on behalf of the town.

"And not just for us," she added quickly. "For them, too."

As repeating words became automatic, she began to see scenes—cooks and maids from the past, polishing silver, ironing sheets, serving biscuits so hot they burned your fingers when you took one from the napkin. Everything was "Yes, ma'am," "No, ma'am," and "Ain't that nice." When she was bad, her nurses never told. "Chile, chile," they said, never unkind. "You ought to be shame." They could crack pecans with their teeth.

Now daughters and granddaughters of the cooks, maids, and nurses stood on Saturday streets with signs around their necks. SHUT DOWN THE TOWN, one sign said, IF IT DON'T DO TO SUIT YOU. Black children ran wild in stores, darted into streets as if daring someone to hit them. Their eyes despised you, not because you were you but because you were white.

Amzi and his followers would take over Wakefield unless something stopped them. What would it be like then?

"People are up to here with this," the white men were saying. "Some redneck will shoot one, and that will be it."

Sally tightened her discipline. Make a mental picture, an expert on prayer had said. Visualize the person well and happy, then frame the picture in your mind. Hold it up to God. She pictured Carter at Market Day on the courthouse square, speaking to people, shaking hands; but the expression on his face was a problem. On the street, in the office, at banquets and rallies, he looked as if he'd been awake all night, worrying while everyone slept. Sally put a smile on his face, made him look happy, then held up the picture to what she thought of as the great ruling psyche of the universe. She held it up until her whole body ached.

For relief she opened a prayer book and turned to the back where a prayer for the sick used to be. It was no longer there, but in the new Ministration to the Sick there were several. "Mercifully accept our prayers," one read, "and grant to your servant the help of your power, that his sickness may be turned into health, and our sorrow into joy." Repeatedly, as in a trance, she read the prayers one after the other, trying to concentrate on the words.

She wanted to look at her watch and see how long she had prayed, but thought it would show lack of dedication. Instead, she brought back the frame, framed the town, and changed the town as she'd changed Carter's face. No picketers with hostile stares. No empty stores. On the contrary, people moving back and forth as busy and harmonious as ants or bees. Faces with pleasant expressions. Sunshine on newly painted houses, little gardens in back with vegetables or flowers.

Up from her subconscious suddenly popped a new scene, just down the hill at the black church, Bethel— Bethel, famous from the sixties when black leaders spoke from its pulpit, shook hands on its porch, stood on its steps while cameras flashed. Now, inside the church, black people were praying for Carter too. Not one at a time as here, but all together, praying and singing in the old way. On the pews elderly black men sat bent over, holding their heads in their hands. Little black girls with

freshly plaited pigtails swung their feet above the bare
floor and looked around with eyes surprised by nothing.
When the choir sang, the others hummed, murmured
"Lord, Lord," or joined in at will. It was music that, if you
heard it as a child, you never got over, because it went
with the nurses who wouldn't tell, with bare black feet,
steaming corn bread and vegetables cooked with salt
pork, with a way of life now gone forever. It went with
people you had loved.

Sally knew the scene for what it was, a daydream of
her own. She wiped it out, framed a healthy new picture
of Carter behind his desk, and held it up as before.

Now and then the frame threatened to get away like
a kite with all the string let out; but she brought it back
each time, back to the center of a clear blue sky where
the eyes of God couldn't miss it. Meanwhile, down below, she moved into a quiet semidarkness without time,
thought, or feeling. All discomfort gone, she slumped
against the altar rail and sank down on the cushion, one
cheek pillowed on the rail.

Arthur woke her with a touch on the shoulder. "Miss
Sally?" His face, looking down, was shocked.

"Oh, God." She came to all at once. "What have I
done?"

"You went to sleep," he said, his eyes wide.

Sally straightened up. She had huddled against the
altar rail so long one foot was numb. Her mouth tasted of
dissipation. The church had a close waxy smell, as in the
hour following weddings and funerals.

"I'm sorry, Arthur," she said. "I didn't mean to go to
sleep. I'll stay on and make it up."

"But you can't make it up, Miss Sally," he said. "You
broke the chain."

Foot dragging, he went to the prayer desk and low-ered himself onto one knee, then the other. He crossed himself, closed his eyes, and shut Sally out.

She stared at her watch as if the watch were to blame. Three o'clock. Three minutes after. How long had she slept? she wondered. Maybe not as long as she feared. Maybe only minutes before Arthur came. It couldn't be as bad as he thought. Arthur was naïve. There was nothing that couldn't be made up, put back together, replaced, forgiven, or sometimes erased alto-gether.

She began to pray harder than ever. Let him live, let him live. She was saying the Lord's Prayer, concentrat-ing on "thy will be done," when the back door opened and someone came in. Someone to relieve Arthur, she thought, without looking up. It had nothing to do with her, for she would go on. Like a jogger into running, she felt she could go on all night.

But the person who came in cleared his throat for attention, and she turned to see Rich standing beside Arthur. Rich had on pants over a pajama top, bedroom shoes on his feet. A quick comb had missed the back of his hair. With one hand on Arthur's shoulder, he looked at Sally.

"I hate to tell you, but Carter didn't make it," he said, and cleared his throat again. "His preacher just called."

Sally gripped the altar rail so hard her rings hurt. Arthur lowered his head and covered his face with his hands.

"They said he wouldn't be the same if he lived," Rich went on. "So maybe it's a blessing."

In the silence that followed Sally got up and tiptoed

past Arthur—still on his knees with his head down—to where Rich stood waiting. Her feet seemed remote from her body, almost beyond her control. Her hands were icy.

"I went to sleep, Rich," she said. "Was it my fault?"

He put his arm around her. "He was doomed from the start," he said. "Nothing we did could have saved him."

When the town clock began to strike, she didn't count the strokes. Whatever the hour, she thought, it was too late. She watched Rich go to the front, bow to the cross, and take a snuffer from its holder. Carefully, an acolyte since boyhood, he began putting out candles one by one.

THE BLACK DOG

My beagle, Little Sister, was in heat when he came, so I thought he was just another male hanging around the dog pen for a few days. I did wonder why my old pointer, Sam, didn't try to fight him off the way he did all the rest.

Country males came and went for miles around, but the black dog was there every morning. He would be lying on the ground outside the dog pen with Sam, or sprawled on the porch, where Sam usually slept on the doormat. He didn't seem interested in Sister.

Anytime I went outside, he ran right up with Sam. No shots against rabies or anything else, I was sure.

"You get away!" I would shout, hoping a shout mean

enough would protect me. Sam would turn back looking hurt, but the black dog only stopped and wagged his tail.

A mixture of pointer, hound, terrier, who knows what, he was almost as big as Sam, but his ears had come out short. One ear was usually cocked, sometimes both, and his eyes never left you for a minute. I thought of him as black, but up close it was obvious that some forebear had been brown. His coat had a definite undertone, like a woman's badly dyed hair. Also, his front feet, plus a large shield-shaped spot on his chest, were white.

Sam would give him a flat, bored look and move away, or lie down and shut him out by closing his eyes.

"Git!" I would yell, each time I went out and saw him. "You git from here!"

It soon dawned on me that he was eating more of Sam's food than Sam was. Sam had chronic nephritis and lived on KD, an expensive, low-protein canned food, which he disliked and was slow to eat. It flew all over him, though, for another dog to get near his bowl. At the age of thirteen he was thin and stiff, with an occasional limp, but still in control of his territory. The way he let the black dog move in was a mystery.

Sam was a purebred bird dog, and also a family pet. My husband had raised and trained him, and both of our children had loved him. Now that my husband was dead and the children grown, I looked on him as the last of the family still at home with me. I also depended on him as a watchdog.

"I could get along without that loud-mouthed dog of yours," the man who read the electric meter told me bluntly one day. "But he's exactly what you need. There's no protection like a big barking dog."

I began feeding Sam on the screened back porch, so Black Dog couldn't get to his food; but Black Dog learned to inch his paw around the edge of the screen door and pull it open. I finally walked out and caught him licking Sam's empty bowl. He was out in a flash, me behind him with a broom. Outdistanced, I threw the broom at him without coming close, but chased him to the far edge of the yard.

"You stay away from here," I screamed. "You *dog!*"

Everything inside me was thumping and pumping. To get a deep breath, I had to lean over. Dangerous, I thought, trying to calm down. I had to go in and sit down to recover.

"I see you got a new one, with a pedigree," Dan the postman teased, when I met him at the mailbox with a letter. Sam and Black Dog had followed, Black Dog standing with one ear cocked as usual.

"I don't know what to do with him, either," I confessed, watching Black Dog's long tail twitch before wagging.

Dan had been on our route for years. When our children were young, they wrote "Hello, Mr. Aultman" on the back of their letters from camp. A problem like mine wasn't new to him at all.

Stray dogs and cats, sometimes lost but usually abandoned, were always showing up on the RFD. It was common practice for people in town to put an unwanted pet in the car, drive several miles down a country road, and let it out near someone's house. The catch was, people in the country have dogs already, work-dogs, watchdogs, pets. The last thing they want is another dog, especially one left on the roadside. And men in the

country have guns, which they use as everyday equipment. When a stray dog shows up with a name on its
collar, the owner is notified and the dog picked up right
away. Otherwise, inquiries are made and a short time
allowed for the stray to move on. After that, a moment is
chosen and a shot is fired, two shots at most.

Dan now propped his elbow in the open car window
and studied Sam's new companion. "He's bad news," he
said. "Want me to bring my gun tomorrow?"

I looked down. It was September and the grass, still
green on top, was turning brown at the roots. "I guess
not," I said. "I don't feed him so maybe he'll move on."

Dan put the car back in gear. "Let me know if you
change your mind," he said.

Now I kept the screen door latched so Black Dog
couldn't eat Sam's food, but still he didn't leave. Under
the hydrant, Sam's water bowl stayed empty half the
time, and water was a must for his kidney disease. For a
while I filled the bowl several times a day, then replaced
it with a bucket.

Late each afternoon I walked with my neighbor,
Anne, for exercise. We met at the edge of my yard and
kept a fast pace down the paved road to an old barn and
back, two miles. The sun put on a show in the west every
day. Around us wide fields stretched out peacefully, as
for the night. Low in the sky, cattle egrets flew in forma-
tion back to their roost. Our walk was a small fixed
pleasure until Black Dog came.

The very first time, he had a paw up on Anne's jeans
before she could stop him.

"You cut that out," she cried, backing away. "Where
did you come from, anyway?"

He wanted to jump up on us and did, if we didn't watch him; so we began to pick up small rocks to throw when he headed toward us. Sometimes we threw as we started out, hoping to stop him from coming at all. Occasionally we even hit him. When we did, he retreated at a halfhearted trot, slowed down just out of our range, and stayed there for the rest of that walk. Next day he was as forward as ever.

Now he was hanging around their house too, Anne said. They didn't feed him either.

Each day began to bring a new complication. I could no longer put out a plastic bag filled with garbage to be carried off later. In fifteen minutes old cabbage leaves, soggy paper towels, and torn cartons full of tooth marks would be all over the yard.

I kept finding the front doormat, chewed up more and more, out on the lawn. A mop disappeared from its place in the fork of a yaupon tree by the back door, a shoe from the front steps. Finally, after an all-night rain, I hung a dress on the backyard clothesline. When I went to bring it in, the skirt was signed with muddy paw marks.

Until then, I hadn't thought of Black Dog in terms of age. He had seemed old, if anything, or ageless; a harassment without past or future except, I hoped, the possibility of disappearing as suddenly as he had appeared. But only puppies and young dogs jump up at clothes on a line. The truth, obvious all along, took me by surprise. Black Dog was only an overgrown puppy, and some of his crimes could be blamed on his youth, which would pass.

Still, I no longer sat under the backyard trees to read the mail when it came, to drink a cup of tea, or watch the birds at the feeder. I dreaded going outside at all because the black dog was there, ready to jump up and paw me, lick me if he could. Weeds grew up in my flower beds. Ivy took over the rock garden.

Anne's husband said such dogs ate rabbits, birds, and garbage, and could go on forever.

One night I invited two couples from town, all old friends, for supper. Greeted by Sam, barking as usual, but with a strange new dog, ears cocked, beside him, they were afraid to get out of the car. Later, at the table, my dog problem became the topic of conversation.

Caroline Jernigan, her salt-and-peppered hair growing out from a short summer cut, said I should take Black Dog to town and put him out in the housing project. People out there wanted anything free, she said. Or I could take him to the pound in Montgomery.

I didn't say so, but I couldn't see myself riding into the project with him, all those eyes on my new compact Buick. Montgomery was fifty miles away, and I wasn't sure Black Dog had ever been in a car, much less how he would behave on the way.

Julia Ames, wearing a peasant blouse and loop earrings, said I should put an announcement on the radio, plus an ad in the paper. "Just say, 'Found. Six miles south of Westwood Christian School, black male dog. Please pick up as soon as possible.' "

"But he's not lost," I said. "He's not wearing a collar, for one thing. And he's never been wanted, you can tell."

"Oh, an underdog!" Julia's eyes lit up. "That's good. That's better. You can say, 'Oppressed minority dog needs good home.' That should fix it."

"No, the underdog here is *me*," I said.

Caroline interrupted the laughter that followed.

"You don't think he'd make a good pet, later on?"

"What about watchdog?" her husband, John, added quickly. John had been my husband's closest friend. "Sam's an old man now, you know."

"Well, this dog doesn't bark," I said. "At least, I've never heard him."

John buttered a roll and put the knife back on his plate. "Let Dan Aultman shoot him," he said. "And forget it."

Black Dog was not around when they drove off, so I put out a feast of table scraps for Sam, everything but meat that he wasn't supposed to have. I was hardly back inside when a commotion, with growls like the start of a dogfight, erupted by the back door. I rushed out, knocked off my glasses on the yaupon tree, stepped on one earpiece, and broke it. But not before seeing Black Dog disappear in the shadows.

In the kitchen stacked with dirty dishes, wearing old glasses through which everything blurred, I gave up at last. Black Dog would have to go, I decided, and the sooner the better. But I was in town seeing about my glasses when Dan came the next day, so I couldn't tell him I'd changed my mind.

That afternoon Anne and I walked by the old Johnson place, as usual. The place had been handed down to a grandson, Bobby Johnson, just last spring. Bobby and his young wife were fixing up the house and cleaning up the lot, repairing, painting, pruning. Doing most of the work themselves. Bobby was at home, his truck parked by the empty garage. Sam and Black Dog veered off into the yard as they always did, sniffing around the shrubbery and the new setter puppy.

Anne and I were hardly out of sight when a shotgun

blast, followed by a row of loud yelps, stopped us. I caught my breath.

"It's not Sam," Anne said, pointing, as Sam came loping up with his tongue out. He dripped saliva on my foot and went on as if nothing had happened.

There was no sign of Black Dog. Our part of the country is generally flat, cleared, and in cultivation; but there are still hedgerows and scattered clumps of trees with undergrowth, where an animal can take over.

"I hope Bobby got him," Anne said, when we turned to finish our walk. She was a gentle person, and her remark somehow shocked me.

On our way back, Bobby met us at his mailbox. He had grown up to be big and serious, a young version of his grandfather, but in jeans, cowboy boots, and a red plaid shirt.

"I hope I didn't scare y'all, shooting like that," he said. "But that black dog has been running us crazy. He eats up the puppy's food and chews up everything on the place. Whose dog is he, anyway?"

"Nobody's," Anne said. "Who would have him?"

"Well, I wanted you to know I didn't hurt him," Bobby said. "That was just bird shot to scare him off."

"Oh," Anne said, plainly disappointed. "I thought we were rid of him."

It seemed that we were, for a while. He was not around my house that night, nor all the next day. Bobby was a godsend, I thought, glad for once that time had marched on. His grandfather would never have bothered with the bird shot.

Undisturbed in my backyard, I drank a cup of tea and enjoyed watching the birds; but a picture of Black

Dog kept popping up in my mind. He was always moving off in slow motion (driven, of course), looking back as if trying to judge the kind and degree of danger. I couldn't help thinking how it would feel to be yelled at, shot at, rejected everywhere you went. Everybody else's bowl filled with food, and no food, much less bowl, for you. I hoped he had found a home and a friend, just so long as the home wasn't mine and the friend wasn't me.

My heart sank to find him, early the next morning, back on my front porch. He had never taken me seriously as an enemy. My screams and pebbles meant nothing to him. Still, when I came on the scene he usually got up and went through the motions of leaving, whether he actually left or not. This time he lay panting through his open mouth, and made no effort to move. His eyes were sad when he looked at me, but he called no attention to his paw, inflamed and swollen, the torn flesh raw and exposed. Bobby's shot had hurt him after all.

Sam was not around. Black Dog was alone on the porch, and I didn't run him off. Instead, I went back in the house and up to my room. I lay down on my bed and stared at the ceiling. What now? I wondered. What to do next?

Nothing, I decided. I would simply do nothing. Since Black Dog was hurt, I wouldn't tell Dan and I wouldn't tell Bobby. But I couldn't afford to help him either. I didn't need, didn't want, couldn't look after, another dog. Each time I left home for more than a day, the dogs I had were a problem and expense, to be taken to town and left at the vet's, where I couldn't get them out again from Saturday noon until Monday morning. I found myself staying at home "because of the dogs." Then there were all the accidents, ailments, shots, and big sacks of dog feed to lug in, in between. No. I could not have another dog, especially the black dog.

When I looked out later he had left the porch, now in full sun, and moved to the shade of a forsythia bush. From this angle, I saw that another paw was also hurt and swollen, though not as bad as the first.

"So that explains it," Anne said, when I told her. "There was blood all over my patio. I didn't know how it got there, but I had to clean it up."

Since he could no longer bother things or come on our walks, he was no longer any trouble. He was just there, sometimes on the porch, sometimes under the shrubbery, sometimes lying in the middle of the road. He would disappear for half a day or a whole day at a time. Each time I hoped it was for good, but he was always back as before.

Sister was now out and about. She and Sam more or less ignored him, and so did I. His feet were getting better, and would heal on their own, I supposed. I didn't let myself think ahead to the time when he would be well again and back in business. "Sufficient unto the day," I decided.

Meanwhile, I was aware of a growing, grudging admiration for the black dog. Hurt and in a hostile world, indifferent at best, he managed to survive without help from anyone. There was something heroic in the way he lay out there alone with his wounds and never, by so much as a look, asked for a kind word or a crumb. I found myself wondering how he did it.

I also wondered why he chose to lie around my house instead of under a tree by Bogue Chitto Creek. Did he want to be around other dogs and people? Or did he know by instinct that amnesty is a kind of victory?

One morning, when Sam and Sister were away, I came across part of a loaf of bread, stale and forgotten in the back of the refrigerator. I had a strong impulse to give it to him but, knowing what it would mean, resisted.

The same night a jolting thud, followed by a few trailing yelps, woke me. The yelps didn't last long and sounded the same as before, so I figured Black Dog had been filching more puppy food and getting more bird shot. Silence closed in again and I went back to sleep, without having waked completely. It was like a dream from which I never really surfaced.

Next morning when I went out for the Sunday paper, Black Dog was dead by the mailbox. He lay full-length on one side, his feet neatly crossed as if running. There was no blood or visible wound on him anywhere, so Bobby hadn't shot him after all.

I couldn't believe he was dead or figure out what could have killed him, until I remembered seeing him lying in the road at dusk and hearing the sounds in the night. He was probably still in the road and a car had hit him. On the blacktop, its headlights must have failed to pick him up in time for the driver to avoid him. But he wasn't bloody or mangled, the way dead animals usually are when hit by a car. One hard lick must have done it.

Deprived of his personality, he seemed smaller than in life, and thinner. Stretched out as he was, full-length in the sunlight, the bones of his rib cage were sharply clear beneath his motley bargain-basement coat. One paw was still inflamed and swollen, bird shot probably in it. The purity of his breast was disarming. Lying there, he might have been dreaming except for his eye, open and fixed, staring up at heaven or back at me.

B E Y O N D N E W
F O R K S

I went to pick up Queen Esther at three o'clock. She was waiting in a chair on the porch, a light-brown black woman of seventy-five, maybe more. She did not know the year of her birth. As I drove up, she put the chair back inside her house and closed the door. She pulled a metal chain through a round hole in the door and corresponding hole in the wall, and turned the key in a lock that held it all together. She dropped the key into a patent-leather purse I had used and passed on to her.

"Get up here with me, Queen," I said, when she reached the car.

"No'm, I'm dipping snuff."

She got in the backseat as she had all her life. Dipping snuff meant she needed to sit by a back window so she could spit without hitting the car. It also meant she had no intention of riding in the front seat with a white person, even me. Her mother had raised us both, me twenty years after Queen, and by the same rules. Now the rules had changed and I had changed, but not Queen.

Tall and still erect, she had on a fresh print dress, a black straw hat, and black Sunday shoes. She smelled of scented soap and starch. Beneath one stocking, tied around her ankle on a piece of string, was the dime with a hole in it that she always wore for luck. In one hand she carried a wooden stick, cut and trimmed like a cane. Accustomed to walking long distances alone, she used the stick to keep off dogs, snakes, and people (she hoped) who might think she had money on her. She also used it to push aside foliage when picking berries or figs, and to hit the limbs of trees and knock down pears, pecans, hickory nuts, and persimmons. She carried it out of habit.

"How far did you say it was?" I asked.

"I told you, Miss. I don't know." There was unmistakable impatience in her voice. "Just go on to New Forks, and I'll tell you where to turn. It ain't that far."

"I just hope she's there," I said.

No response. She did not want to go. I'd known all along but found it hard to believe. Lou Annie was her grandchild, named for her mother, whom she called Ma and I called Mannie. Mannie had been my nurse and, before and after that, had worked in our house all her working days. My earliest memory, pinpointed like a snapshot, was of standing up in a baby bed, holding on to the side, with Mannie looking on.

It was late October. So many trees were bare that my house, built by my great-grandfather's slaves, was partly visible from the road as we drove by. There were no other houses on the farm now except mine and Queen's. The land, the whole thousand acres, had been leased to soybean farmers ten years ago, the cabins sold for the lumber, tin, and bricks in them. Black people bought the cabins, tore them down, and put them back up on small plots of land of their own.

Only the empty shell of a cotton gin, almost hidden by bushes and vines, and the six-columned Greek Revival house itself were evidence that the farm had once been a so-called southern plantation.

The grounds of the house needed all kinds of attention. I had had no yardman in years. A white boy from town came out to mow the grass in summer. During graduate-school vacations my two sons tried to prune shrubs, rake leaves, and burn trash, and my daughter cleaned out old flower and bulb beds. But they always had exams to study for and papers to write. Occasionally I found someone to cut and haul off dead limbs, undergrowth, and honeysuckle vines, but there was no such thing as actual maintenance anymore. Now and then I went out alone and worked all day.

"Lou Annie can live up with me, in the old cookhouse," I said to Queen. "Or down there with you, if you want her. You ought not to be down there by yourself."

"I been down there twelve years by myself," she said. In the rearview mirror I saw her eyes fixed straight ahead, her jaw set.

Whatever was wrong, I didn't take it seriously. Queen was temperamental, but her "heart" had always been, would always be, her one child (called Son by everyone, black and white) and his offspring, whom she called "grands" and "great-grands." Lou Annie was her favorite grand, or so I had thought.

For one thing, Lou Annie looked so much like Mannie. Mannie must have had strong, dominant genes, since they all favored her and each other: Queen, Son, the grands, even the ones who were black like Son's wife.

But the likeness was most striking in Lou Annie. In Mannie's lifetime we never thought of black people as pretty, but I knew now that Mannie was, with her gentle features and *café au lait* coloring. Lou Annie had inherited hints of her face and bearing, but especially her amber eyes. In all my memories of Mannie, it was the eyes, haunting and intelligent, that came back first and faded last. Each time I saw Lou Annie it was like seeing Mannie, in a youth I never knew.

"How's your garden?" I asked Queen.

"Ain't nothing in it but a few collards," she said, as though letting out the sentence and slamming a gate behind it.

So I gave up on conversation and kept my thoughts to myself. I had decided to offer Lou Annie a full-time job if, at the minimum wage or some kind of salary, I could afford her. My house had been built with servants in mind, and servants were now a thing of the past. Even part-time help on an hourly basis was hard to find, usually incompetent, sometimes barely polite.

"Would you turn out the lights when you come downstairs, please?" I would ask with careful deference.

The answer would be "Yeah" or "Okay," occasionally "I will." Anything not to say "Yes, ma'am." But hours later, if I didn't check, lights would be on, dust under beds, cobwebs still in corners.

My children (all still unmarried) came home at will, often with guests, expecting fresh sheets on the beds, good food on the table, and the unwavering support of a rocklike parent. Now that a blue shield-shaped Historic Home marker had been put on the porch, there were more visitors and visits by groups. Pilgrimage years were traumatic.

In the front-hall mirror, framed in gold leaf and needing Windex, I began to see a wraithlike widow, hurrying back and forth, shoulders hunched forward, eyes teeming with worries.

Queen understood, I thought. She was by birth, and also by choice or default of choice, as much a part of it all as I was. Either of us could have left anytime after we were grown. I did leave, in fact, to return with a husband who ran the farm for the rest of his life. Queen never left at all. She had moved once, from the house in which she was delivered by a midwife in Mannie's iron bed, to the one where she lived with Isaiah.

"You don't suppose she's moved, do you, Queen?" I asked.

She rolled down the window and spat. "No'm, she ain't moved."

"How long since you've seen her?"

"I disremember."

"Then how do you know she's still there?"

"I keeps up with her, that's how. You just go on, and quit worrying."

Queen grew up in our kitchen, my mother said, sweeping when the broom was taller than she was, standing on a stool to stir bowls of batter, helping the cook, who was never Mannie. Mannie refused to cook but had full charge of the housework.

Queen became a superb cook, cooking full-time for us, three meals a day, while still a girl. Unable to read or write, she did not use "receipts" but cooked, as she said, by taste. She did not taste from the stirring spoon (having been told, no doubt, not to), but spilled a few drops on what seemed to be an asbestos palm. Once on her tongue, the taste was examined behind a forehead usually beaded in sweat. With a closed look in her eye and brows knit together, she made small staccato smacking sounds with her lips while deciding what a little more salt, pepper, or a tap of sugar would do. In our world she soon had no peer.

Over the years her job reduced itself to two meals a day, and finally one. She was cooking midday dinners for me at the time she hurt her back. Attempting to move a wood stove in her house one winter afternoon, she cracked a vertebra. From the hospital Son took her to his house to recuperate, a matter of months, the doctor thought. Son and two of the grands came to get the rest of her clothes and her trunk.

"Mama have to retire now, and stay with us," Son said, stopping by to leave the key to her house. "But she be up to see you when her back get better."

"Well, I should hope so!" I said. "You tell her she can be retired up here as well as she can down there. The house is hers. Let her keep the key."

One day at noon, a few weeks later, my dogs began to bark the way they bark when the children come home.

From the kitchen window I was surprised to see Queen walking up the back lane. She held herself a little straighter and stiffer than before and used her stick for support. But she looked fine, considering.

"Just in time!" I said. "I've got a good dinner, all ready."

But she shook her head. "I come to tell you I'm back in my house."

"You mean, to *stay?*"

"I can't live in no house with Fanny." Fanny was Son's wife, her daughter-in-law.

"How's your back, though?" When she left, she could hardly get up and down, much less bend over. "Are you *able* to stay by yourself?"

"My back just as good as it ever was, only yet weak," she said. "Thank God."

She never mentioned coming back to work. She had served her time, we both knew, and then some. Besides, I no longer needed a cook for the simple food I ate alone, and she was inevitably failing. What I needed now was a strong young cleaner.

If I had a company meal she helped out, then put on a uniform, and served it in style. When the children were home, she came up to fry chicken, make biscuits, or cook someone's favorite. Otherwise, she stayed at home and did as she pleased.

With Son's help she built a hen house and began to raise chickens. She pieced quilts for the grands, grew vegetables and flowers, made gallons of wine from muscadines, scuppernongs, and berries.

We kept casual check on one another, visiting once a week or so, on her porch or under my trees in summer, by her fire or in my kitchen in winter. We went through our memories like ragbags from which each drew the scraps that pleased her. Sometimes, intent on the big design our scraps made together, we ignored or even altered details.

"Son never gave you a minute's trouble," I might say one day, wiping out entirely the time he ran away and stayed a whole year. It put her to bed for days at the time, sick, crying, lying for hours with her head beneath the quilt.

Again, for no reason, one of us would insist upon the literal truth. "No'm," she would say, all of a sudden. "I walked to Dr. Mason's that day."

"You *walked?* Well, I know Daddy would have taken you if he'd known you had to go."

"Yes'm, but I walked."

It was four miles to Dr. Mason's and four miles back. He found a large fibroid tumor to be removed from her womb. She called it the Fireball.

And suddenly the whole Pandora's box of race, with all the unconscious, unintended, even unrecognized withholdings of respect, status, privilege, even rights we never thought about, much less understood at the time, embedded as they were in custom and usage, would open up to silence us completely.

We never tried to examine or explain such things in words, as some claimed to do. We would simply look at each other helplessly, after which one or the other would change the subject and start getting ready to go.

As we neared New Forks, Queen leaned forward on the seat. "Yonder at the filling station is where you turn," she said.

So we left New Forks off to the right and turned onto Highway 80 itself, which went on east to Savannah. With only two lanes along here, the road was dangerously inadequate. Accidents were so frequent it was known as Bloody 80. On each side freshly harvested soybean fields were interspersed with dairy pastures, where cows grazed hard for a little green beneath a lot of brown.

"Tell me where to slow down," I said.

"Just keep going," she said, and leaned back.

Small ranch-style houses, approached by gravel lanes beginning in cattle gaps, sat back from the highway. Occasionally there was a larger, older frame house, usually in need of paint, whose entrance was lined with cedars or crape myrtle. This country was not what my husband used to laughingly call "The Old Magnolia South." It could be Anywhere, USA, except for Negro houses along the way, houses nicely painted or covered in siding of imitation brick, in colors sold as "buff" or "rust." Each house had two rooms and a porch, an over-riding TV antenna, and one or more cars, bright with chrome, parked in front.

"See that colored church?" Queen pointed up ahead. "After that, watch out for a dead tree and a dirt road. That's where you turn."

The church was of raw, red brick, with a modest steeple and windowpanes marbleized in green, blue, and purple. The sign in front said GOOD HOPE BAPTIST CHURCH. On one side a newly fenced-in cemetery was so thick with headstones it seemed crowded already. Almost every grave had a wreath or spray of artificial flowers in fading rainbow colors.

My hands were suddenly wet on the wheel. Without help I could no longer maintain, for long, the status quo at home. But there was more to it than that, something nonrational and emotional. I was looking for more than a maid to wax the floors (though the floors indeed needed waxing). In my heart I was looking for another Mannie or a young Queen Esther. Lou Annie was my last hope, I knew.

Queen once talked of her all the time, then stopped completely unless I asked. She had finished high school and married. When her husband left her with two children, she went to work in a small clothing factory in Orrville, forty miles away.

"Is Lou Annie still at that plant?" I had to ask.

"No'm, she in a café now."

"In Orrville?"

"No'm. Safford."

"What does she do—cook?"

"You know she can't cook. She waits on peoples."

"Does she like it?"

"She likes them tips."

I soon came to expect new jobs in different towns for Lou Annie, but one day Queen's answer took me by surprise. She was helping a white lady in Selma, Queen said.

"Doing *housework*?" I looked up from the peas we were shelling together. "Is she satisfied with that?"

"Seem to be."

The peas in my lap were forgotten. "Do you think she would ever come and help *me*?"

Queen's eyelids went down like shades at the close of business hours. "You have to ast her that," she said.

But when I began to press for a time to ask, she kept putting me off. First Lou Annie was away from home, in Birmingham. Then she had a new job, in a motel. After that, Fanny had the high blood and she was at home taking care of her mother.

One day I happened to meet Son on the street in town. He was delighted by my interest in Lou Annie. He bet she would come to work for me in a minute. It was where she ought to be, he said. Back home.

"Is that the tree?" I asked Queen. A large dead pine was up ahead. Just beyond it, a dirt road led off to the left.

"That's it." She sat forward on the seat. "Slow on down."

It would be muddy here when it rained, I thought, as I turned onto the exposed gray soil. Driving carefully, I tried to straddle the multiple ruts, deep and dry now, that ran close to and parallel with the highway. Beer cans, discarded cigarette packs, and limp paper bags were strewn along each side as though Lou Annie's house might be a store where such things were sold, or a neglected public park.

The house itself was neither painted nor sided like those we had passed. It looked more like the ones we had torn down at home, after having stood vacant for years. Everything about it needed jacking up and fixing.

"Don't go too close, Miss!" Queen said.

So I stopped at the outer edge of a bare yard criss-crossed with tire tracks. Another car and a pickup truck were already there, parked near the porch.

Two children, a boy and a girl, were playing out front. They turned to look at us, did not recognize Queen, and showed no further interest, as if strangers were commonplace. The boy clutched a squirming kitten to his chest.

"I'll go see if she's there," Queen said, hunting for the handle that opened her door.

"I'll come with you," I said.

"No'm." She was positive. "You stay here."

She got out, in her hat and Sunday shoes, the patent-leather purse swinging from one hand, and I watched her walk through what seemed a wall of soul-rock music. As she passed the children, she leaned down, smiled, and touched the girl on the head. She might have been a stranger on the streets of a city.

Going up the steps, she paused to put a staying hand on each ascending knee, but once on the porch she straightened up, crossed the narrow space, and knocked with authority on the door to one room. When no one came, she waited briefly, went to the door of the other room, and knocked again. Almost immediately Lou Annie opened the first door.

She had on a pink tank-top and a short, tight, flowered skirt. Her bare feet were in Jap Flaps. Her hair stuck out in an unkempt natural state. At the sight of her grandmother, she attempted to straighten her skirt with one hand and close the door behind her with the other.

At the same time the other door opened and a black man, naked from the waist up, looked first at Queen, then at me in the car, and disappeared as suddenly as he had appeared. Both Queen and Lou Annie ignored him.

I watched Queen point and explain about me to Lou Annie. Then they started slowly out to the car, Lou Annie in front and Queen behind her, looking down.

I was out now, standing beside the car. "How are you, Lou Annie?" I asked.

"Okay," she said, and waited.

Her skin, once a smooth, glowing brown, seemed thicker and coarser. She was thin now, instead of slender as before. Muscles stood out on her upper arms and calves. The tight skirt revealed a slight potbelly.

I looked from her to Queen and back. "I've been needing someone to help me in the house, Lou Annie," I said. "Your grandma and I came to offer you the job."

"Y'all did?" Her brows drew together in a frown.

A large transfer truck was going by on the highway. We could feel its vibrations, smell its hot, acrid breath. It stopped conversation and drowned out the music, but the beat throbbed on.

Lou Annie turned to the children and raised her voice. "Girl, go tell them folks to turn that thing down!"

Both children ran to obey, then came back to stand and stare at us. We were not ordinary visitors after all, it seemed. We had stopped the music.

"Grandma didn't know I already have a job," Lou Annie said, in the quiet that followed. "I'm just here today since it's Sunday."

A disturbed blue jay, with raucous cries and reckless wings, lit in a tree nearby. Branches shook, leaves turned loose to fall, and he was gone. Several leaves, carried by a cold, rising wind, fell at our feet.

"Well, I'm disappointed, Lou Annie," I said. "I really need someone. I'd pay as much, or more, than anybody."

But the look on her face did not change. There was no considering, wavering, or doubt. Her refusal was as final as the passing of the truck, and our business was over.

Queen leaned down to the dirty little girl.

"How you, ba'y?" she asked kindly. "You don't remember Grandma Queen?"

The child stared at her with blank, opaque eyes, and shook her head, no. But the little boy brightened.

"I does," he said.

"Does you, boy?"

Queen opened her purse and took out a white man-sized handkerchief in which something was tied up. Hastily undoing the thick knot, she withdrew four coins, and handed two to each child, the boy first.

"Keep that, now. Don't throw it away," she said. "It's from Grandma Queen."

She opened the car door and got in.

"I'll bring 'em to see you sometime, Grandma," Lou Annie said. "You be sweet."

"Be sweet yourself, girl," Queen said, and slammed the door.

I paused before getting in. "Well, Lou Annie," I said. "Think of me if you ever do need work, or anything. I feel like you're one of the family."

"Yeah?" she said, and her amber eyes despised me.

I had trouble starting the car, then turning around. She stood and watched. The children leaned against her, playing with the coins in their hands.

"Les us take notice now." Queen sat up on the edge of the seat as we came to the highway. "I'll help you look."

"Good," I said. "Thank you."

She knew I was upset, and she didn't want me to pull out in front of a big truck and kill us. We looked carefully both ways. Safely on Bloody 80, we headed home in silence.

"Well, I tried to stop you from coming," she said, after a while. "But you hardheaded."

"I know," I said. "I was set on it."

"Don't forget where to turn."

"I won't. I remember."

The filling station had seemed closed when we went down, but now it was open, doing business. Someone was buying gas and someone else came out drinking from a can. I saw the Cold Beverages sign.

"Want a can of beer, Queen?" I asked, knowing how she liked alcohol of all kinds. "It might help us."

"Yes'm," she agreed at once. "Sho might."

I forgot about Sunday blue laws and went in to ask for a six-pack. The filling-station owner gave me a second look, put the beer in a sack, and said nothing. I went back and handed the sack to Queen.

"Go ahead and have one," I said.

"No'm," she said. "I'll wait."

I drove slowly, my hands dry now. The road home seemed lonely, leading back to the past instead of on to the future, like a half-forgotten scene in some old grammar-school reader. On either side flat fields, newly harvested, lay serene in the quiet light. Low in the west, the sun was going down in flamboyant red and gold.

"Look at that sunset," I said.

"Yes'm," she said. "Sign of fair weather."

At her house we got out, and I waited while she unlocked the chain and opened the door. It was cold now, almost like winter. A drift of dry, brown leaves had collected on her porch.

"Come on in, Miss," she said, and turned on a hanging light bulb in the small room she papered with fresh newspapers each spring.

A fire dozed in the fireplace. She poked it with an iron poker, put on a piece of wood, and pulled up a chair for me. I opened the sack, twisted two cans from the plastic holder, and handed one to her. Sitting close to the hearth, we pulled the tabs from our cans. She took a deep swallow.

"Ain't no use to be sick, Miss," she said. "She's just a whore, that's all.

"But, my God, Queen!" I said. "*Why?* She was so smart, and pretty."

"It ain't no excuse." She looked directly at me. "She don't want to work. Don't none of 'em. And she likes that kind of a life, drinking, dancing, smoking that pot. Sleeping all day and carrying on all night. It ain't no excuse."

In the fireplace small flames danced together like a chorus line and began to really burn. I unbuttoned my sweater and pushed back my chair.

"Well, she's not the only one, Queen," I said. "My children are no angels. They drink, and smoke dope too, right upstairs, and think I don't know. And who knows what else they do when the boys bring those girls home."

She said nothing.

"My own child is living with that boy, I'm afraid," I went on.

"She told me she wadn't never going to marry that boy, though," Queen said. "Nor nobody else."

"I'm not surprised. Did she say why?"

"Said she loved her freedom too well."

"And that's just it. . . ."

But I couldn't go on. There was no way to talk about this, like race. It *was* race, actually. One of my sons was in his last year of medical school, the other on the law review at the university. My daughter would never be a whore. Thinking it, knowing it, only made me feel guilty, and worse.

We watched the fire in silence.

"Don't look so pitiful, Miss," Queen said, at last. "I'll come back up there and help you."

I stared at her speechless for a moment. She thought I was thinking only of myself, and still she said it, meant it.

"No," I said quickly. "I wouldn't let you do that. All that bending, stooping, up and down stairs? No ma'am!"

She looked down to the can in her hand, gave it a small, rotary shake. She had offered and I had refused. It was all we could do for each other.

"I'll just have to make adjustments," I said. "I could shut off the upstairs and live downstairs. I could even rent out the upstairs."

I tried to imagine the shutting off and renting. It was like putting the wrong coin in a dispensing machine.

"What I ought to do," I said rashly, "is lock it all up, and go hunt another husband."

Suddenly Queen laughed, a laugh so spontaneous and loose I couldn't help joining in. Halfway serious, I had not meant to be funny and the laugh was on me; but the dark spell was broken, if only for a moment. Fading smiles were left on our faces.

"Here," I said, holding out my unfinished can of beer. "I don't want this."

"I does," she said. "I'll drink it."

I stood up to go, first checking the pictures on her mantel as I always did. We were all still there, crowded together. Jesus and Martin Luther King were in gold frames and in color, one on each side for balance. Everyone else was propped against the wall or each other, in curling snapshots cracked with age, recent Polaroids, glossy school prints, and posed studio portraits in cardboard folders: black people and white people in her family and mine.

I put my arms around her. Like Mannie, she accepted but did not return my displays of affection. She did not open her arms, for instance, and hug me back but only patted lightly with one hand.

In my embrace her flesh gave way and the bones beneath felt bare and brittle. Old. She freed herself as from a child, and opened the door.

"Done got dark out there," she said.

"It's all right," I said. "I've got a flashlight in the car. Shoot the gun if you need me. Shoot two or three times, so I'll be sure to hear."

"Yes'm. You do the same."

At the top of the steps, I paused to look back at her. "Don't give up on Lou Annie," I said. "Something will turn her around." Suddenly I spoke with a passion and conviction that surprised me. "When their time comes, I expect them all to stand up and do right!"

"Yes'm," she said, letting me have the last say, as Mannie had taught her. " 'Night, 'night."

But I had forgotten to put a flashlight in the car, and there was no moon. When she closed her door there seemed no light anywhere in the world except in the headlights of my car.